I0554213

In Name Only

by

Sarita Leone

A Willowbrook Manor Romance

This is a work of fiction. Names, characters, places, and incidents are either the product of the author's imagination or are used fictitiously, and any resemblance to actual persons living or dead, business establishments, events, or locales, is entirely coincidental.

In Name Only

COPYRIGHT © 2015 by Sarita Leone

All rights reserved. No part of this book may be used or reproduced in any manner whatsoever without written permission of the author or The Wild Rose Press, Inc. except in the case of brief quotations embodied in critical articles or reviews.
Contact Information: info@thewildrosepress.com

Cover Art by *Debbie Taylor*

The Wild Rose Press, Inc.
PO Box 708
Adams Basin, NY 14410-0708
Visit us at www.thewildrosepress.com

Publishing History
First Tea Rose Edition, 2015
Print ISBN 978-1-62830-799-3
Digital ISBN 978-1-62830-800-6

A Willowbrook Manor Romance

Lucie had read the letter so many times the paper was soft, and creased, from being handled so often. The words were committed to memory, but she could not resist opening the missive and reading his sentiments again.

My dear Miss Gregory,

It is my most sincere wish that you had as pleasant an evening as I did. Why, it seems barely possible that we parted just hours ago. I admit I find myself already missing your company and looking forward to our next conversation. It may be indelicate to state my feelings, but I warned you that I am not one to beat about the bushes. I would rather be rebuffed for my honesty than strung along because I am playing a part.

I have never found the rooms at Almack's as intriguing as I did yesterday evening. Your company brought wit and charm to the otherwise-stifling atmosphere. You were a vision of sunshine and enchantment in your gown. Being by your side reminded me of being gloriously out-of-doors beneath a warm July sun. I was charmed by your beauty and countenance.

Thank you for spending your evening with me. I hope I did not wear out your slippers, or your feet, with my endless walking. If I did, I will replace them, of course. (I mean your slippers are replaceable, not your feet.)

I plan to call at Willowbrook Manor in a few days' time…

Dedication

Love never dies.

Chapter 1

London, June 1814

"Straighten your shoulders, Lucinda Jane. You don't want some impudent man peeking down the front of your gown when he asks for a dance, do you? Gracious, my dear, sometimes you have less sense than a goose!"

Lucie dutifully pulled her shoulders back so her gown's low-cut, yet oh-so fashionable pearl-trimmed bodice lay snugly against her chest, exactly where its dressmaker, as well as Aunt Lucinda, believed it ought to be.

Had Lucie realized how wholly involved Aunt Lucinda, the Dowager Countess of Waltham, would become in every facet of her dress and behavior, she might not have agreed so readily when her aunt offered to sponsor her for the Season. But she had not known, so she had accepted the proposal. Now, she had to take the sour with the sweet, and smile when she might have otherwise wished to stamp one dainty, slippered foot.

As the crowd inside the ballroom at Cresthill, the Earl of Gloucester's London home, grew, so did the heat. The air would have been utterly stifling had it not been for the staff of frond-waving servants placed strategically around the huge room. Still, as the dancing progressed, breathing easily grew increasingly difficult.

Lucie snapped open the delicate, handmade silk fan that hung from a ribbon at her right wrist. The fan matched her gown perfectly, its aquamarine hue chosen by Aunt Lucinda to show Lucie's creamy complexion to its best advantage.

At the moment, Lucie doubted her complexion was creamy at all, or even the tiniest bit becoming. She felt soaked in perspiration, and even though she knew her aunt would be vexed by the request, she could not hold off any longer.

Turning slowly, not wishing to appear indelicate and further displease her aunt, she gently waved her fan in front of her lips. "Aunt, I am nearly wrung out with the heat. I fear I must take a breath of fresh air, and quickly."

The older woman cast a dubious gaze at her, the heavily powdered skin around her eyes wrinkling disapprovingly. Her expression spoke volumes. Lucie had no doubt that "back in the day" neither Aunt Lucinda nor any of her friends would ever have been so frail they required air—fresh or otherwise.

"Really? Why, I rather feel the touch of a chill." With a dramatic shiver undoubtedly designed to squelch the request, Aunt Lucinda pulled the fine silk georgette shawl at her shoulders tight with one gloved hand. Its dark green edging and fringe matched the feathers on the dowager's headdress.

Lucie stood her ground. "Be that as it may, I could nearly swoon from the heat. Either that or the boned corset you and your modiste insisted I wear is far too tight. My lungs feel deprived of air, and unless they are refreshed in all haste, I am sure I will fall to the ground. Just think…if I swoon here and now, and crumple helplessly at your feet, all kinds of improper peeks down my bodice might—and most likely *will*—be stolen."

She slapped her fan closed, leaned in close to her aunt's ear and whispered, "Oh! Imagine the scandal."

Aunt Lucinda blanched, giving Lucie a perverse pleasure she immediately felt sorry for having. She was grateful for her aunt's care and concern. The gowns and other essentials that had been provided—at great expense—were all of the best quality and made Lucie one of the most fashionably turned out women of the Season. Endless balls, musicales, and theatre openings had not only entertained but let Lucie gain entrée into salons and ballrooms she might never have seen otherwise. No, she had no desire to give the impression she was anything but extremely thankful for her aunt's time and energy.

Lucie was in Aunt Lucinda's debt, but being obligated did not mean she must put all of her own thoughts and needs completely out of her head, did it? Especially when the most pressing need was for one of the most basic of human requirements.

"Very well, if you must," her aunt said with a deep sigh.

Lucie remained firm. "I must."

The crowd converged mainly on the dance floor, so the area just in front of the open French doors leading to the wide stone terrace was clear except for a pair of servants who held silver refreshment trays. Aunt Lucinda glanced at the doorway, and at the refreshment trays, before she turned her attention back to her niece.

"Take a friend. Or two. How about your friend Amy, the one who is always giggling about something or other? And her sister…what is her name…?"

Aunt Lucinda tilted her head toward her right shoulder, and the plumed headpiece she wore tucked into her coiled upswept gray hair leaned in an alarming manner. Lucie watched, wondering if the peacock feather would slip out of the hairdo, but it did not. It waved, swaying with each movement of Aunt Lucinda's head.

Relief at her aunt having kept her hairdressing intact swept through Lucie. "Her name is Miranda. But Miranda is dancing with the Earl of Chatham, see?"

She nodded discreetly to the center of the room where her friend bobbed and dipped in the arms of a tall, gangly man whose feet were so large they disappeared beneath the hem of Miranda's gown with every step.

Lucie stifled a giggle of amusement at having seen Miranda's plight. She knew how difficult it was to avoid the earl's toes; she had been partnered with him about an hour earlier, and her own feet still bore the imprint of his fine leather footwear. The only consolation was that the dance was nearing its end. Soon Miranda—and her toes—would be free of the earl.

"Well, find Amy, then. I don't want you walking about on the terrace unaccompanied."

"I am perfectly capable of taking a few breaths of fresh air without a chaperone. I have been breathing since the moment of my birth, you know." She smiled, hoping to lure some of the starch from her aunt's demeanor. Beneath the rigid exterior lurked a fun, and often very amusing, woman. The trick, Lucie knew from experience, was to coax her aunt to let herself be her true self, without worrying overmuch about what others might think or say.

Tonight was not the night for letting down one's guard, apparently. Aunt Lucinda frowned, and then said, "Don't sass me, miss. I helped your mother change your swaddling clothes, and you are not so big I have forgotten how it felt to hold you in my arms. I have earned the right to tutor you on the finer points of gentility."

"I know you have, Aunt. I apologize for my impertinence."

Her aunt waved the apology away with one hand. The rings she wore on top of her gloves sparkled in the lamplight, sending scattered reflections of color dancing onto their outfits. The effect was magical, and Lucie was momentarily captivated.

"Pish posh, Lucinda Jane. I know you are a spirited young woman who can take care of yourself in almost any situation. We have taught you well, your mother and me. It's just that here, at such an elegant affair, I do not wish you to appear unschooled." She leaned close and took one of Lucie's hands in her own. Giving a fast squeeze, she said, "It would reflect badly on me, you know, if you were to speak or act out of turn. So, I am forced to admit, I am protecting my reputation as well as yours."

The rigors of society! Why couldn't they all be set aside from time to time, if only to allow a bit of excitement and freedom now and again?

That will never happen, Lucie thought. There is no freedom for an unmarried woman. And after marriage, how much freedom can one possibly hope to find?

The situation seemed hopeless, so she pushed

thoughts of doing what she wanted to do, when she desired to do it, from her mind. Instead, she focused on her most pressing need—fresh air.

"I understand." She returned the hand squeeze, and then extricated her fingers from the older woman's grasp. "And I promise not to cast any doubt on your ability to properly—and more than eloquently—show me the ins and outs of appropriate deportment. I will find someone to accompany me onto the terrace." When her aunt opened her mouth again, Lucie realized her mistake. "Someone *suitable* will accompany me, I promise. Listen, the music is just ending. If I hurry, I may be able to take Miranda's arm and lead her out-of-doors with me."

She turned to walk away, but her aunt had the final word. "Just a short turn about the terrace, mind you. I do not want you to miss the start of the next waltz. I do believe your dance card is nearly filled from this point forward, my dear. It wouldn't do to keep any of the *ton's* eligible bachelors waiting, now would it?"

Of course it wouldn't, Lucie thought with a shake of her head. It wouldn't do at all to seem uninterested in securing a match. That is why we are all here, isn't it? Trussed up like Christmas geese so tightly we can barely breathe—and all to snare a husband.

Lest her aunt engage the servants on a full-scale hunt before Lucie had a chance to restore herself, she took the time for a reminder. "The next dance is not a waltz, dear aunt. It is a cotillion. I am, thank heavens, without a partner for it, so I shan't be missed if I do not return before the opening chords are struck."

"Cotillions *aren't* your forte, are they Lucinda Jane?"

The barb hardly mattered, for it was the truth. Waltzes were her strongest talent on the dance floor, followed closely by the various other popular dances. The French cotillion, with its complex steps and ever-changing round of dance partners, was the downfall of many dancers. Lucie was no exception. She was relieved not to have to make her way through the intricate moves of the night's cotillion.

She suspected there were many others who felt likewise.

"No, they aren't." Manners brought a small smile of false regret as well as a rueful sigh. "You know as well as I that the idea of dancing a cotillion put me at sixes and sevens. I get the collywobbles at the idea of following—or not being able to imitate—the lead couple in that dance. No, it's much better for me, and my reputation—as well as *yours*—if I don't attempt a cotillion."

Aunt Lucinda opened her mouth, and for a moment looked like a carp out of water gasping for air as she tried to form a reply to the impertinent comment, but Lucie impulsively bent forward and kissed the woman on one powdered cheek. The skin felt papery beneath her lips, a reminder that her aunt was no longer a young woman.

Overcome with gratitude and love, Lucie repeated the gesture before she pulled away. Smiling brightly, she said, "I promise to practice my dance steps. Who knows? Perhaps by the time the next ball comes around I shall be so proficient in dancing the cotillion I will be the first woman in the room to have her dance card filled."

Delight made the older woman's face look years

younger. Dreamily, she said, "Wouldn't that be grand? Oh, Lucinda Jane, we can only hope…"

Smiling as she turned for the door, Lucie thought, Yes, we all need to hope for something, don't we? You may hope for overflowing dance cards, Aunt. As for me, I shall keep my hopes for other purposes.

****

Lucie furrowed her brow. "Miranda, whatever are you doing? And please, do whatever it is as quickly as possible. If Aunt Lucinda sees, we shall both be in trouble."

Miranda cast a furtive glance to see if anyone was watching before she placed her right foot higher up onto a marble ledge. She pushed her gown aside, leaned down, and massaged the tip of her dancing slipper.

"Oh, that man and his big, clumsy feet. I nearly screamed aloud—more than once—when he stomped down on my toes." Miranda moaned so pitifully it was difficult not to feel sorry for her. "How can a man so totally lacking in dancing skills and with such enormous feet be such a coxcomb? He is so vain and conceited, it is almost beyond belief."

Commiseration, spoken softly so they wouldn't be overhead. Lucie said, "I know. Why, when he sent me flying across the dance floor earlier, me trying to avoid his down step at every beat, all he could think to discuss was his vast store of sovereigns, bundles of government securities, and his stable filled with priceless horseflesh. When he wasn't trying to impress me with his wealth, he went on about how well he sat a horse and what the ladies said when he gave an exhibition of his fine riding ability." The memory made her laugh quietly. "I know it is uncharitable of me to say so, but I was never so glad to hear the final notes of a dance as I was when I danced with him."

"I second that feeling." A small snort, so unladylike it was completely out of place on the elegantly decorated terrace, followed the comment. "And to think, I only danced with him out of sisterly obligation."

Miranda straightened. She patted the fullness of her heavily embroidered overskirt, smoothing it down over the deep blue satin gown she wore. The color and design suited the redhead to perfection. Blue was Miranda's signature color, matching her eyes and setting off her hair to its finest display.

Had Lucie not loved Miranda, and Amy as well, like her own sisters, she might have been envious of their exotic coloring and beauty. But she was not prone to wanting what she could not have. Her own looks were more than adequate and had served her well in the past. She assumed they would continue in the same vein for, at the very least, the foreseeable future.

"What do you mean, 'sisterly obligation'? What does Amy have to do with your choice of dance partners?" Lucie pulled her eyebrows tight and tried to puzzle the meaning behind the words.

Miranda peeked about, again looking to see whether they were alone. Lucie followed her lead, her gaze flitting across the empty space surrounding them. There were several darkened nooks and corners on the terrace; occasional whispers and giggles came from the murky shadows, but they were far enough removed from any of the niches to need to worry about being overheard—or overhearing anything themselves.

Pulling Lucie close, Miranda whispered, "I danced

with the earl so Amy could have a private word with Lord Lyle Roark. It has been ages, though, since they slipped away. Oh, I do hope my dear sister is not off somewhere raising a breeze. Whatever will Mother say if she finds out I have allowed this to happen? If Amy does step out of line, it will certainly set up Mother's bristles. Mark my words; there will be the devil to pay if something goes awry." Miranda twisted her fingers together, pushing her gloves askew and giving them wrinkles they had not had a moment ago.

"I am sure Amy is fine. Your mother need never know she slipped away. Goodness knows, only you and I are privy to her secret, and we will not give her up, will we?"

"Perhaps I shouldn't have taken her place so willingly. Perhaps she and Lyle…"

"Nonsense." Lucie refused to think her friend would have any judgment save good, proper judgment regarding her dealings with men. Besides, Lyle Roark was a peer. His manners, breeding and regard for women were above reproach. "Lyle would no sooner besmirch Amy's reputation than…than…why, I can't even come up with a comparison, it's so preposterous to even consider the matter. No, you did them both a fine turn by dancing with the earl. Who knows? Amy may be so relieved at your having saved her toes she might be willing to do you a good deed in exchange."

Miranda looked unsure of the matter but managed a small smile. "You may be right. I just hope my sister has enough sense not to be caught doing anything untoward. Amy is always ready to kick up a lark, you know. Sometimes I wonder that we can be sisters. She is too ripe and ready by half and here I am, more bluestocking than party girl."

"What sense is there in comparing yourself to Amy? Your sister is her own person, as you are yours, dear Miranda. Neither of you should yearn to be the other."

Lucie had often wished for a sister of her own, someone with whom to share silly secrets and discuss the future and the promises it held for them. But perhaps the most sincere part of her longing was the simple wish for a sister who would hold her hand during the casual events of life, rub her shoulders when she cried, and share laughter until their sides ached and tears dripped from their chins at any farce too funny for Lucie to bear on her own.

All the wishing had been for naught. Lucie was never blessed with a sister to confer and giggle with. Instead, she had one brother, Oliver. At four and twenty, he was two years her senior. Their lives had intersected, but they had never been particularly close. Lucie loved Oliver, and she knew he felt likewise, but theirs had been paths that led in divergent directions. Since her brother had never seemed the type to giggle, hold hands or share confidences, the arrangement had suited both quite well.

Her circle of friends, and especially Miranda and Amy, had admirably filled the void where a sister might have been. It had been some time since Lucie had gone to sleep after wishing on a star in the night sky with a sister on her mind.

"You are right, I suppose." Miranda smoothed a palm down the front of her gown, wiping away the pleat above her knee left by her holding her foot within massaging distance for so long. "I should be more concerned with my dance card." She opened the tiny book which dangled from her wrist. She shook her head. "It is mostly empty, I am afraid. If someone doesn't take a fancy to me soon, I may be forced to hide out here all night long."

"Oh, don't be such a cake! You cannot possibly see any names on your dance card in this darkness. Who can read in such dim light? No one, that's who."

Flickering torchlights gave the only man-made illumination on the terrace. Set at intervals designed to provide both some semblance of decorum while strollers took the air as well as secluded, dark corners for the more romantically inclined to steal a kiss or secure a promise, the torches were not suitable for reading by.

"I don't need candlelight in order to know what this dance card says. It is dismally apparent I am more at home between the pages of a good book than on the dance floor. And to further underscore the fact, my dance card reminds me of that truth. It is, I fear, nearly desolate. Only three dances are spoken for."

It was not Miranda's lack of breeding or beauty that made her less in favor than other young ladies. It was not her intelligence, either, that put men off. Several men had been intrigued by her extensive array of facts, her understanding of politics, or her ability to see the solution to a problem long before others had grasped the idea a problem even existed.

Miranda's sparse dance card was due in large part to the way she did nothing to encourage suitors to get to know her. When a man—any man, even one whose wit and intelligence matched her own—approached, Miranda was more likely to examine his appearance the way she might observe a rare insect specimen stumbled upon during an afternoon nature stroll.

In short, Miranda examined men, and their motives, the way naturalists looked at creatures beneath their microscopes. No man, sincere in his affections or merely intrigued by her genius, had thus far been able to endure the close, almost paralyzing, scrutiny Miranda doled out.

Both Amy and Lucie had spoken with Miranda about her putting men under her imaginary quizzing glass, but their efforts had been wasted.

It was not Miranda's dance card that concerned Lucie now, but her own. She murmured absently about being sure Miranda's would fill as the night progressed, all the while thinking of the gentlemen who had scribbled their names into her own small book. It, like the fan, dangled from her wrist. But unlike the fan, the tiny tome felt as heavy as the piece of marble her friend had so recently rested her sore foot atop.

All the names in the book belonged to men who were, on the surface, respectable. Most were kind, handsome, and reasonably well-off. It was the case with nearly every gentleman in the ballroom.

The cream of society's crop had been invited to the night's festivities, leaving every eligible female in London desirous of an invitation. Not all had received one. Fortunately Lucie's impeccable family line, and Aunt Lucinda's sponsorship, had left no doubt that she would be one of the privileged invitees. But now that she was here, Lucie wondered if all the hoping, and hoopla, had been for nothing.

Make no mistake; the evening was all some might wish for. Still, dancing with men who held little or no fascination grew tiring. Despite Aunt Lucinda's prodding, no one had garnered Lucie's affections. She had yet to meet the man who might make her pulse race, her heart hammer, or her blood boil. While she had never felt any of those things, she had read Miss Jane Austen's *Sense and Sensibility, A Novel by a Lady* and knew such glorious feelings were possible.

Miranda's hand on her elbow brought Lucie back to the moment.

"I should go inside and see if I can't track Amy down before Mother begins searching for her."

"Good idea." They took a few leisurely steps toward the open French doors. New music had not yet begun so she knew she would be forced to endure watching the upcoming cotillion while Aunt Lucinda stood beside her and pointed out every one of the finer points of the dancing couples.

"I should get back to my aunt before she does the same for me."

"May I escort you inside?"

A smooth-as-silk male voice broke into the conversation. Lucie had only heard it once before. A week earlier she had been introduced to the man who spoke now, presumably to either her or Miranda, at a charity luncheon by the sponsor of the affair, Lady Clare Winters.

Their meeting had been brief, but he had left a very definite impression on Lucie's mind.

She turned.

Manners had been instilled since birth, so Lucie effortlessly dropped into a curtsey while at her side Miranda did the same. Their sudden guest bowed, and she noticed how sleekly his hair gleamed in the torch's lights.

Nicholas Grayson, the Duke of Waterford, appeared almost too well-groomed, too good-looking, and far too dashing to be real. His handsome elegance impacted her heart, and she felt the first fluttering of tightness in her chest. Either her whale-boned corset had been tied too securely, or the duke's devil-may-care smile, square jaw line, and darker-than-midnight black curls made her lose her breath in one unladylike *whoosh*.

His eyes. They are as I remembered, Lucie thought with amazement. Exactly as I thought they were…

The most startling part of the duke, aside from his appearance seemingly out of thin air, was his eyes. So dark they were almost black, they seemed to see right past Lucie's face and straight into her soul. She felt exposed beneath his gaze, despite the way he tempered his study with a rakish smile. Even that, the grin he bestowed upon her, was brilliant. Each tooth dazzled, and seemed to bring light to the darkness.

"Lord Grayson, what a surprise." She returned his smile, willing her heart to stop beating so erratically in her chest. How on earth could a man—*any man!*—have such a disconcerting effect on her?

"A pleasant surprise, I hope."

"Of course," she murmured politely. Turning and pulling Miranda close beside her, Lucie brought her friend into the conversation. "You remember Lord Grayson, don't you, Miranda? We met at Lady Winters' luncheon, the one to benefit the Orphans and Widows Home. Remember?"

"Yes, of course." Miranda said nothing further, not even after the duke inclined his head in her direction and greeted her pleasantly.

Lucie got the feeling her companion was studying the handsome man as if he was a striped caterpillar plodding along the leaf of a maple tree. She could have elbowed Miranda, just to get her talking, but it would have been too obvious a gesture. There was no way to poke her, so Lucie merely grit her teeth and made a mental note to discuss, yet again, how best to carry on a conversation with a man.

"Would you allow me the pleasure of partnering you in the upcoming cotillion, Miss Gregory? I have already enquired with your aunt, who informed me that your dance card is empty for the cotillion. It would be delightful if you would do me the honor of allowing me to be your partner." His words sent both a chill of horror as well as a tremor of excitement up her spine.

He leaned close, so close Lucie caught a whiff of the spicy scent of his aftershave lotion. "I must confess, I have a particular fondness for dancing a cotillion. Please say yes."

Lucie's mouth said "yes" but her mind wanted to scream otherwise.

And her feet? Had they not been clad in butter-soft slippers which were wholly improper footwear for any activity other than dancing, they would have run so fast and hard it might have looked like the gates of hell had been thrown wide and all the ghouls, demons, and tortured souls let loose…and on Lucie's trail.

Chapter 2

Slim fingers of sunlight danced across the coverlet. They peeked into the room through the sliver of light showing between the heavy damask draperies covering the windows in Lucie's bedroom at the family estate, Willowbrook Manor. She shifted, and a beam of warmth touched her chin, her nose, and finally her eyes.

Opening one eye and turning toward the window beside her bed, Lucie tried to gauge the hour by the height of the sun. It was barely visible through the drapery crack, so she guessed the time to be quite early.

Listening for activity confirmed her assumption. There were footsteps in the hallways and upon the stairs, but they belonged to servants. The difference between feet trying to remain undetected and those who took creating noise as their due for owning the place upon which they trod was drastic. The sound of footsteps was faint, and scurrying, and could only belong to maids carrying coal or wood for the fireplaces.

The warming pan beneath the covers near her toes had gone cold long ago. Lucie touched its metal lid with one toe, and then pulled her foot up beneath her nightdress. Although it was June, nights could still be damp and chilly inside a manor as old and drafty as theirs, so warming pans were provided every night of the year.

Willowbrook Manor had been in the Gregory family for generations. With wide, stone walls and two turrets, it looked more castle-like than manor-ish, but whatever the style, it had served the family well over the decades. Just outside the city, it was set smack-dab in the middle of a sprawling, forty-acre plot of land. Rolling meadows, forested areas, and a spring-fed pond made the estate seem almost magical. A caretaker's cottage, stable, and various guest houses dotted the landscape.

It was close enough to Town to be convenient yet far enough removed that the family could feel completely cut off from the rest of the world if they so desired.

Oliver was next in line to inherit the place when their father passed on. Lucie hoped it would be years before that eventuality became reality.

Lord Gregory had been frail since he began having what his doctor termed "vapors" but which Lucie suspected might be a chill stuck in his lungs. Both she and her mother had urged the lord to journey to Bath, to take the waters, but he had resisted. Lucie was convinced that drinking or bathing, preferably both, in the mineral waters would heal her father, but he was nothing if not stubborn, and had steadfastly refused her urging.

Today I shall entreat him again to take the waters. If not at Bath, then perhaps at Tunbridge Wells. Doing practically anything is preferable to simply taking no action. Yes, I will try once more to make him see reason, and do what is in his own best interest.

Lucie stretched, scowling up at the white lace bed canopy above her head. She loved her father dearly, and the notion that he preferred to grow more ill rather than fight whatever it was that ailed him annoyed her. If she had to, she would use her secret weapon, the one Father had never been able to resist.

If all else failed, Lucie would cry. She hated to do it, but her father had never been able to deny her anything when she had a tear upon her cheek. To heal him, she would cry bucketsful of salty, wet tears if forced to do so.

A woman had to use whatever means were at her disposal to see her way clear in the world, even if it meant reddening her eyes and running her nose. Yes, she would do whatever it took to help her father regain his health. Nothing was more important than the family—and no deed too distasteful.

He should be in the pump room at Bath, she thought with renewed resolve. He should be drinking the mineral waters, taking snuff with the other gentlemen, and talking horseflesh. Yes, that is what he needs, a good stretch at Bath...

She had absolutely no intention of allowing her father to stick his spoon in the wall at this point in his life. If he insisted, he could up and die when he was a very, *very* old—practically ancient—man, but not before. Not if Lucie had anything to say about it.

Throwing aside her covers, she swung her legs over the side of the bed and onto the stepstool. She rested for a moment before she stood up and descended the wide mahogany steps. When her feet hit the floor, she shoved them quickly into her bedroom slippers. June or not, the old wooden floor was ice-cold.

Only in England do we wear furry slippers in the summer, she thought with a shiver. I bet in other parts of the world the floors are warm.

Lucie pulled her wrapper from its hook and stuck her arms into the armholes with more force than necessary. Her smile disappeared when she remembered it did not matter how hot—or cool—floors were elsewhere. She was stuck in England, and it was nearly unimaginable that she would ever see anywhere else in the world.

Traveling? The lord believed travel was the realm of men—and *only* men. Oliver had gallivanted around the continent several times, but Lucie, whenever she asked to go anywhere, had been denied the privilege. Two years ago, she had gotten wise to her father's way of thinking and had simply stopped asking.

But she had not lost the desire to see the world beyond England, and this morning's chilly reminder it would likely never happen rankled her.

There was no sense lamenting over what could not be changed, so she took her comfort, washed her face and brushed her teeth, all the while thinking about the dance. She could not get the affair off her mind—not that she had any desire at all to do so. No, reliving some of last night's events, if only in her own head, was something she planned on doing all day long.

It had ended so much more splendidly than it had begun. Evenings at Cresthill were never dull, but last night's fete had closed on such a high note Lucie thought it just might be the most unrivaled affair the earl had ever hosted in his grand home.

A short rapping on the door caught her attention. Most days the family breakfasted together in the morning room, but on mornings following parties, Lucie sometimes requested a tray be brought to her bedroom.

Ida Mae, in a starched black-and-white uniform complete with cap, entered carrying a large tray. The scent of orange scones, Lucie's favorite, wafted into the air and made her mouth water.

"Good morning, miss."

"Good morning."

The maid walked on silent feet into the room and went straight to a table beside the window. She placed the silver tray on the gleaming tabletop, then turned and pushed back the heavy draperies. Sunlight streamed unencumbered into the room, filling it with brightness and warmth.

"Looks to be a fine day, miss. Or at least it might be, once the sun chases away the nip in the air."

Ida Mae had been at Lucie's disposal for only a year, having replaced the former ladies' maid when that young woman had been called home to care for her aged mother. It had been hard to see Gwendolyn go, but there was no stopping a daughter when she felt compelled to assist a family member. Dedication to one's family, especially when that family found itself in dire straits, was an admirable trait. She had given the young woman a bag of castoff clothing for her own use, a bundle of old-but-still-serviceable linens for the family's needs and a small, yet weighty, coin purse and wished her the best.

It had taken a few weeks for her to grow accustomed to her new help, whose mannerisms and language were somewhat less animated than she was accustomed to. She was, however, a fully competent lady's maid, and either anticipated all requirements or rushed to satisfy them when they were made known. If she had any fault, it was simply that she was not Gwendolyn. And as far as Lucie was concerned, one could hardly be chastised for being oneself rather than someone else.

Lucie was, aside from her wistful longing to travel, a pragmatic woman who made the best of, and enjoyed to the fullest degree, every moment of every day. She had learned to accept whatever came her way. On most occasions, she did so with a cheerful disposition.

Flashing the maid a smile, she seated herself at the table and arranged her dressing gown to cover her ankles. It would not do to get a chill now, not when the Season actually held some promise of excitement and intrigue. Last night had changed everything. It was impossible not to smile like a satisfied cat that had just filled its belly with a bowlful of heavy cream. It took all her effort not to *purr* her contentment.

"You are right; it does look like it will be a pretty day." She unfolded a white linen napkin and laid it across her lap as she surveyed the items on the breakfast tray before her. "I believe I will take a walk after breakfast."

"Certainly, miss. I will assemble your walking costume. Do you have a color preference today, or will any morning dress and pelisse do?"

She liked choosing her own clothes, so frequently she did so rather than allow someone else that liberty. It was a small gesture, but in a world where so much seemed dictated by the rigors of societal customs and the remainder by familial structure, it was something she could control. Besides, she had enjoyed dressing her dolls in fancy clothing and daring colors when she was a child. Now she could have even a small hand at doing the same for herself.

"I believe I'd like to wear the yellow—no, the lilac dress the dressmaker delivered last week. I'm not sure I'll need it, but please make certain the matching pelisse is unwrinkled, as well."

The day might be too warm by the time she finished breakfast, but if it was not, she would love the chance to wear the complete ensemble. Made from silk so sheer it felt like a whisper on her body, the lilac outfit had caught her eye the moment she and Aunt Lucinda walked into the dressmaker's shop. With a few simple alterations, it fit so well it looked custom-made. She did not have a mind to impress anyone with her appearance, because the morning would surely pass without her seeing anyone but the family and servants, but dressing sharply had a way of making the day brighter by far. She smiled, wondering how on earth this day, which had already filled her with warmth and happiness, could possibly get any brighter.

Practicality won out over the desire to wear the entire ensemble.

"Oh, as much as I adore them, I will not wear the lilac slippers with the dress. My walking shoes will do."

The obligatory curtsey. "As you wish. Ah…will you desire the fichu that arrived with the morning dress? It is a lovely lilac lace, and would make the outfit much more…ah, seemly."

Vigorously Lucie shook her head. She had not wanted the fichu in the first place. Her aunt insisted on it, so that was the reason it arrived with the pretty outfit, but having it in her dressing closet and actually wearing the ridiculous thing were two entirely different issues. The scrap of lace which fit into the bodice of the dress and extended up the slope of her chest was designed to afford an extra layer of modesty.

Granted, there were times when dresses were so low cut that their occupants' endowments threatened to topple over the upper edge of their bodices, but the lilac dress was definitely not *that* low cut. In fact, none of the gowns in her closet were designed to over-expose her in any way.

A fichu was something Aunt Lucinda believed belonged with every dress, but Lucie disagreed. She would rather wear a suitably-cut dress and forego the affectation. In her view, it only pulled attention toward the area, so rather than preserving modesty, it put the neckline in the spotlight.

And despite Aunt Lucinda's objections to her not wearing a fichu with every dress she owned, Lucie had never worried her modesty might be in jeopardy. She was nicely built, but there would never, ever be any fear she would wear something so low-cut that she might spill over the top of her dress. She was far too modest and practical for the concern to be warranted.

She drew her eyebrows together and looked at the waiting maid with a groan of distaste. Shaking her head, she reached for the cozy-covered teapot. "No. Please hide the thing somewhere in my closet where it will never be discovered. Better yet, gather up every fichu you can find in there and give them to the downstairs maids to use as dust rags."

Steam rose from the cup of tea she poured. The scent of roses and chamomile whetted her appetite. Last night she had hardly eaten. Now she was glad for the heavily laden food tray, sure she might consume every single morsel.

"You can't mean that, miss. Dust rags? Why, it would cause a scandal below stairs!"

Lucie broke open a scone and slathered honey on it. Waving her free hand in the air beside her head, she said, "No, no…I am only wishing aloud. Do not donate my fichus to the parlor maids; just please leave them somewhere I am not likely to spot them. The lilac dress, its matching pelisse, some stockings, and my brown walking shoes are all I require. Thank you."

"As you wish, miss."

A loud squawk from the far corner of the large room reminded them there was another present, one who wished his identity immediately revealed. A second squawk, followed by a flapping sent Ida Mae scurrying across the floor. She removed a square white drape from atop a birdcage, revealing an enormous green-and-blue parrot.

"Good morning, Cedric," Lucie said. She tapped her tongue against the backs of her upper teeth, making a clicking noise to which the bird instantly responded. When he answered with a *click-click-click* of his own, both his mistress and her lady's maid giggled.

"He is such a lark." The drape was folded and hung over the back of a low chair beside the birdcage. "Meant for the stage, I think. This bird would recite Hamlet or play Macbeth if he could speak properly."

"Speak properly." The parrot bobbed his head as if he agreed with every word that came from Ida Mae's mouth.

"I said 'speak.' Not 'mimic'—there *is* a difference, you know." The maid wagged her index finger at the bird, taking care not to waggle it too close to the wide-set bars of the big bird's cage. His beak was as yellow as the sun, but not nearly as welcoming. It had been known to nip many a careless finger—a lesson the maid learned her first morning serving Lucie.

"Oh, you speak just fine, don't you, my dear Cedric?" Lucie motioned for the parrot to be brought closer, so Ida Mae carefully picked up the cage with its attached metal stand and brought them nearer the table. "Thank you. Now we can linger over breakfast together. Isn't that right, my friend?" She offered a bit of toast which the bird promptly took in his beak.

"Linger." The word was somewhat garbled due to the toast in his mouth.

The women shared a swift moment of amusement before Ida Mae remembered her place and, with enough starch in her voice to please even the Queen Mother herself, enquired, "Will there be anything else?"

"No, that will be all for now. Thank you." Lucie swallowed her own toast, brushed her hands across her napkin, and then offered a polite smile.

Her parents had taught her from childhood that just because the household staff was in their employ there was no reason for her, or anyone else, to treat them with less than utmost courtesy. If she had even entertained the notion—which she certainly never had—to be slightly high in the instep, her parents would have given her a severe dressing down. Haughtiness and false pride were not tolerated in Willowbrook Manor, neither from the family nor its staff.

Lucie had still been on leading strings when she learned that very valuable lesson. It was one she had never forgotten.

With a proper curtsey, the maid said, "As you wish."

She walked to the door and opened it. There, poised upon the threshold and about to knock, stood Miranda.

"Oh! However did you know I was here?" Miranda asked as she stepped into the room. Ida Mae curtsied a greeting to the visitor, and then backed out, closing the door behind her. "Your mother is downstairs in the morning room with your father. She said I should come right up. I hope it is all right…"

Beckoning her over to the table, Lucie grinned. "Of course it's all right. Why, there is even enough breakfast for you on the tray, and an extra cup and saucer as well. Come, sit beside me and we shall chat about last night's fun."

"Last night's fun?" Cedric's questioning squawk stirred them both to laughter.

Miranda removed her pelisse and dropped it on the back of a chair. They hugged, the way sisters might, and Lucie was reminded yet again how wonderful it was to have such a dear friend. She might not have a blood sister, but she had her sisters-by-friendship, and they more than made up for what she did not have by birth.

"I could not wait any longer. I just had to hurry over to see how you feel this morning." Miranda sat, accepted the cup of tea offered her, and with familiarity borne of countless shared meals, took a scone and buttered it. She took a bite, closing her eyes at the taste and rubbing her midsection. "I am famished. I do so wish women could eat whatever they desired at these affairs. Why, oh why, do we have to deny our hunger and wave the food trays off? It is no wonder so many women swoon at parties. Between our corsets cutting

27

off our air supply and the emptiness in our bellies, it's a miracle we have enough energy for dancing, isn't it?"

In answer, Lucie pushed the scones and butter dish closer to her friend. She knew where the conversation was headed…

As if on cue, Miranda continued, "Ah, yes…the dancing. Why, the dancing was something else entirely, wasn't it? I mean, the music…the starlight on the terrace…the cotillion…"

At the mention of the cotillion, twin blooms of heat rose on her cheeks. She placed the second half of her scone back on her plate. Her appetite had suddenly disappeared, the empty feeling in her tummy replaced by a fluttering completely unfamiliar to her.

She lifted her teacup to her lips, and then paused without taking a sip.

"The cotillion…" Miranda evidently had no fluttering at all in her, because she finished her second scone and held her hand open in contemplation above the quickly emptying plate. It took only a second for her to decide; she helped herself to a third scone with a small toss of her hair.

"You *do* remember the cotillion, don't you? Oh, you are wool-gathering again, aren't you? Or perhaps you have lost your taste for chatter with the likes of me. So dull by comparison to the duke, I'm sure," she teased.

The jolly words brought Lucie's thoughts back to the breakfast table. It was true. She had been indulging herself in the glorious memory of last night's cotillion.

"I could never consider you dull." Lucie took a swallow of her tea, and then placed the delicate china cup down on its matching saucer. There was no reason not to be forthcoming. She shrugged, admitting what she could not hide. "I did let my mind wander. I apologize, but I could not help myself. It was such a fabulous, amazing evening, wasn't it?"

Pushing back from the table and crossing one leg over the other, Miranda looked less impressed by the memory. "I cannot lie, not even to make you happy. The evening was passably pleasant for me, at least if you discount the earl and his big, stomping feet." She grimaced.

"Ah, the earl's dancing. I had forgotten about that."

"Of course you would, given the fact that you have something infinitely more enticing and certainly much less stressful on your toes to remember than I do." Miranda pulled a face, wiggled the tips of her shoes and laughed.

The good-natured banter brought a word from the parrot. "Toes!"

"That's right, Cedric. Poor Miranda's toes were damaged in the dancing. Don't we feel like crying over them? Her poor, sweet, squashed toes…"

"Squashed toes!" He was rewarded with a small bit of Lucie's uneaten scone, gobbled greedily from her fingertips.

"All I got last night was a round with the biggest feet in London, while you, my dear, were swept across the dance floor in the arms of a man who outshone every other man in the room. In the whole of the City, I imagine, there is nonesuch as he."

No argument to counter the claim formulated in Lucie's mind. She merely sighed, and nodded her head in agreement.

"Yes, I did feel as if I was floating on a soap

bubble when we danced the cotillion. He held me so firmly, and led me so beautifully, it was impossible not to dance as if my feet were under his spell, and needed no guidance at all from me."

She paused, cocked her head to the side and chanced a quick look at the slippers peeking out from beneath the hem of her robe. "Highly unusual, don't you think? I have never felt such complete confidence in anyone's arms save…"

Lucie considered a moment, and then shook her head when no name popped into her mind.

She finished, "Well, I suppose I have never felt such unrivaled confidence when held in anyone's arms—except Lord Grayson, that is. He inspires confidence, don't you think?"

Miranda gave an exasperated sigh. "He inspires a walk—that is what I think. Come on. Let us get you dressed so we can ambulate about the rose garden. Maybe the scent of late-blooming hyacinths or early-blooming peonies might be enough to clear those smoky wisps of last night's dance from your head."

When Miranda reached for the small silver bell on the table, Lucie shooed her hand away.

"No, I can dress myself. I have already decided what I shall wear this morning, and I am certain Ida Mae has everything already laid out for me." She stood and took a few steps toward the door before she turned back to face Miranda. Pointing to the last scone on the tray, she said, "Why don't you finish them off? You know you love them as greatly as I do, and since my stomach seems to be suffering a fit of nerves, you may as well do the honors for me. Come on, pour yourself another cup of tea and nibble the scone. If you do not mind, I am sure Cedric would enjoy another bit of toast. I will be back in a tick. Maybe two, if I cannot easily manage the buttons myself."

Lucie headed for the dressing room with her friend's words firmly in her head. Miranda was right. What she needed was some nice fresh air, something ordinary and pleasant that would clear her head and chase away the mist that clung stubbornly to the inflated memories of dancing with Lord Grayson. Surely the event couldn't have been as magical as she believed…could it?

She was nearly dressed when she heard a crash from downstairs. The sound was followed by a scream, then another crash. Lucie ran into the bedroom where Miranda stood, her view out the window so engrossing she did not turn at Lucie's approach.

"What is it?" The sound of scuffling, loud voices, and more crashing brought the need to raise her voice. She ran to the window and peered out. A carriage was parked outside. The team of horses which had pulled the closed conveyance was lathered and sweat-slicked. They had apparently ridden hard, probably through the night if the dust on the carriage was an indication of the miles recently traveled. "Whose carriage is that? I do not recognize it."

"I don't, either. And I did not see who alighted, since I was not aware of its presence until the shouting began." Miranda shivered, her distress evident by the frightened look in her eyes when she turned to Lucie. She noticed Lucie's buttons were undone, so she moved to stand beside her and began buttoning the lilac silk closed. "I heard hoof beats, hard and fast, but I just imagined it was someone to see your parents. I knew it could not be a delivery because the carriage stopped out in front, but I did not presume to intrude. It did not occur to me to come to the window and stare out. Your parents are certainly entitled to receive visitors without my sticking my nose where it does not belong."

Miranda's habit of chattering when she was in a state kicked into high gear. If she was not stopped, or at the very least her fear forestalled, she might become fatigued to the point of fainting. Or just as disagreeable, she might lose the contents of her stomach. Since Lucie had seen how fully her friend's stomach had just been stocked, it was in her best interest to squelch Miranda's emotions—as quickly as possible.

She turned and took Miranda by the shoulders. The other woman trembled violently. Lucie felt her trepidation so completely it could have originated in her own body. She gave Miranda a gentle shake. If the mild movement did not do its trick, she would have no alternative but to issue a soft slap across the other's cheek.

Resorting to force was something she did not want to do but, like tears, sometimes one was pushed to use the devices at hand, and those that worked best.

But first, a second slight shake.

"Please get hold of yourself. You are working yourself up into a lather that is nearly as distressing as the horses' by the door. Why, you're shaking so hard I can almost hear your teeth chatter."

She wished she still needed her buttons done up. At least when Miranda's hands had been occupied she had not had them clenched so forcefully they were white from the pressure.

"Miranda! Do you hear me? Get control, now.

You're frightening me." It seemed to do the trick, because the frightened eyes focused on hers, and she gave a small shake of apology.

"I-I am sorry." Her teeth still chattered but her gaze seemed clearer. "I've never been one to endure shouting. And...and there seems to be such a great lot of it, doesn't there?"

There was a preponderance of raised voices, as well as intermittent crashing and the sound of things breaking. It was distasteful at any time to witness— even from a distance—some kind of ballyhoo, but with Miranda present, it was far worse than it might have been otherwise.

Amy and Miranda's parents, Lord and Lady Spencer, endured one of the unhappiest marriages in England. Their daughters had been subjected to hearing, as well as seeing, marital battles which had left their mark on each one in her own way.

While Amy's outgoing, cheerful nature and strong desire to find a suitable man to wed, and live with happily ever after, encouraged her to dance, date, and flirt with every eligible bachelor in sight, Miranda had been otherwise affected by her parents' matrimonial disharmony. She abhorred discord of any manner and was more likely to be found with her nose in a book than engrossed in discussion with a man. When even the tiniest scuffle erupted in her presence, she took flight like a frightened house mouse, seeking a safe, cozy spot in which to hide until the conflagration resolved itself.

It was patently clear the commotion downstairs had her tied in knots.

"Calm down." Lucie wanted nothing more than to

take the stairs two at a time and see what was going on, but she could not leave her friend in such a fragile state. Smoothing Miranda's curls away from her face with her hand, she spoke loudly enough that she hoped she drowned out at least some of the noise making its way up to her room. "You look nearly done to a cow's thumb, and it is probably nothing to raise a flap over. This is not your parents' house, sweetie. It is Willowbrook, and here there is never anything happening worth shaking so badly over."

Miranda managed a feeble smile, her lower lip trembling dangerously.

She knew the look. If she was not careful there would be tears—great, fat, rolling tears—to follow. It was too early by far to deal with waterworks. Besides, she had yet to discover the cause of the disturbance.

Curiosity needled her, so she ran a hand over the row of buttons on her side below her arm. "Thank you for doing me up. I do not believe I would have been able to do it on my own. Lud, but these buttons get smaller every Season, don't they?"

The distraction worked. Her companion shook her head agreeably, raising her own left arm in demonstration. "They do at that. Mine look like miniature pin heads, don't they? My Abigail had a terrible time with them." She dropped her arm, giggling nervously. "Who knows? Maybe next Season *The Lady's Magazine* will proclaim large, clumsy, easy-to-fasten buttons all the rage. Wouldn't that be something?"

"We can hope so." Lucie had one ear on the commotion and the other on their conversation. Neither got the attention it deserved. With a mind to extricating herself and checking downstairs, she gestured to the tea tray. "Why not have another cup of tea? I will just dash down and see what is up, then fetch you so we can take that walk. How does that sound? What do—?"

Before now, the sounds reaching them had been a jumble of noises and voices. Lucie had not been able to sort them out. Now, one voice thundered above the others.

It chilled her heart.

"Be gone! Be gone from this place while there is still time! We are—"

The words ended abruptly, replaced by a heart-wrenching wail that raised gooseflesh on her arms. She knew the voice, and the man who owned it.

Oliver had arrived at Willowbrook Manor, and he sounded wholly tortured.

Chapter 3

It did not matter that Lucie would have preferred staying at Willowbrook Manor instead of attending a lawn party given by Lady Claire Blakely, Aunt Lucinda's daughter-in-law and the current Countess of Waltham. Her aunt's insistence that she be present at the heretofore highly anticipated event took precedence over Lucie's feelings.

The country home, Waltham Hall, lay just outside London proper, not far from Willowbrook, and retained many similar features to those at her own family home. As such, she should have felt somewhat mollified at being there, and less out-of-sorts than she did.

The truth, in plain, unvarnished terms, was that she felt as nervy as a cat in a room full of rocking chairs. She wanted nothing more than to climb back into the phaeton which had conveyed her to Waltham Hall and head straight back to Willowbrook. She would have done so, too, had the chance to flee unnoticed presented itself. It had not—yet—but her senses were sharpened for any and all prospects of flight.

Alas, her wants were inconsequential, and any mention of her unwillingness to partake in the day's festivities brought a wave of reproach from Aunt Lucinda so, for the present, Lucie kept her own counsel. Eventually there would be an opportunity for escape. For now, she did what any well-bred, polite young lady would do—she smiled when she wanted to screech, and laughed when she felt like crying. Most importantly, she pretended to enjoy herself.

When she let herself forget feeling betrayed by circumstance and the expectations of society on her gender, she relaxed a little. Not enough to fully enjoy herself, but her guard dropped and her mood lightened passably.

Miranda noticed instantly and took the moment when Lucie first sighed her acceptance of her situation to invite her to stroll the grounds.

"Shall we take a turn around the lawn? Perhaps pinch a bloom or two from Lady Blakely's roses?"

Miranda gave her an impudent grin, more reminiscent of a toddler than the smile of a grown woman. The gesture was spirit-lifting.

Why not enjoy herself as best she could? The day was lovely, with a cloudless blue sky. A whisper of a breeze slipped coolly from the surface of Waltham Pond, and made the air around them feel soft as silk.

It would not do to waste a day—*any* day—even when what she wanted was drastically different from what was provided.

In a wheedling tone, "Come on, Lucie. You cannot stay in a miff all day long. It is too nice a day for such a long face. A walk will do us both good, I think."

With a nod, she accepted the invitation. They left their folding seats beneath the trees beside the terrace and headed for the rose garden. It was distant enough that a stroll would be private, but not so far from the crowd that they would not be observed.

Before they reached the rosebushes, Lucie got straight to what was bothering her.

Oliver had been at Willowbrook Manor for two days, yet she had not been allowed to see him. It cut her to the quick that she was being kept from him. Her parents' explanation for the separation was logical, but she sensed something more behind their story.

"Oliver is staying in the cottage near the brook. At least, I am pretty sure that is where he is." Lucie wrung her hands at her waist, her fingers tied so compactly that had they been made of thread the knots they formed would have been unbreakable. "Mother and Father refuse to allow me an audience with him. I think it's reprehensible that he's being kept from me—I *am* his sister, after all."

Miranda looked uncomfortable, but she did not try to change the topic.

"Perhaps they have a very good reason for keeping visitors at bay."

"I am *not* a visitor. I am his sister. *His sister*, by God!"

Goodness, where had her hard-headedness come from? She had always considered herself someone who could see, and understand, both sides of an issue. In the past, that had been the case, but now, with the current situation adding unheralded tension to Willowbrook Manor, all she could think to do was to see her brother, and somehow fix whatever ailed him.

It was apparent he suffered from something…something highly unfortunate, possibly contagious and, for all she knew, virulent and deadly. If only her parents would give her some information about his condition, she would feel less tortured.

"Yes, you are his sister." Had Miranda not been so bent on staying out of scuffles at any cost, she would have made a fabulous negotiator. Smoothing stormy waters came naturally to her, and the soft, almost hypnotic tone of voice she reserved for times such as these could calm the most high-strung being. "But Oliver might need rest—and silence—in order to heal properly. I am sure that when he is well enough, they will let you see him."

A lump appeared in her throat, threatening to cut off the space between her head and her heart entirely. Lucie swallowed hard. Tears pooled in her eyes, burning in their saltiness. She blinked once, then twice, before she spoke.

She hated the way her voice sounded, so choked and forlorn, but there was no helping it. "I don't know if he is going to get better. I...I...oh, I just don't know..."

They had reached the rose garden and walked along the wide, grassy rows between the formal lines of plants. The scent was both intoxicating and somewhat overpowering, depending on which variety of rosebush they passed.

Only the fear that someone might pop out from between one of the lines of rosebushes kept Lucie from letting her tears fall. She knuckled away the first, and only, tear that escaped with a little sniff.

"Are you saying what I think you are saying?" Miranda stopped and turned to face her. With eyes as wide and round as saucers, she lowered her voice and asked, "Are you saying you fear Oliver may...that he might...well, do you think he may not recover?"

As much as she hated to do so, she nodded her head. It seemed perverse, but the admission of her deepest, darkest fear was marginally satisfying. It was only a small relief, but every bit helped.

"That is exactly what I think." Lucie's voice came out strong and steady, the conviction of her heart giving her words substance. She turned back to the path and began to walk slowly, Miranda keeping pace step for step.

She had speculated on Oliver's condition since the morning he came home, raving like a lunatic and thrashing around so dramatically that several expensive art objects had been smashed in the front foyer. Of course, she had not witnessed any of the outrageous actions first hand. By the time she dashed to the stairs and ran to the spot, he had been led away. All that remained of his appearance were shards, a broken table, a white-faced butler, and her parents, both of whom looked ready to drop.

What could make Oliver behave so erratically? Usually calm, rational and highly intelligent, he was a man to whom his peers looked for guidance. He was genial, and even though they had spent long stretches of time apart due to divergent school schedules, then Oliver's stint in the King's Army, they had maintained a friendly, loving relationship.

Nothing in all her years of being his closest blood relation prepared Lucie for this sudden—and most heartbreaking—development.

"What do you think is wrong with him?"

Her friend had once set her cap on Oliver, but it had been years earlier when she had first come out. He had paid her hardly any attention at all that year, or any time afterward. Lucie suspected Miranda was considered an unsuitable match by Oliver solely because of their close friendship. It might have been difficult—nearly impossible, even—for Oliver to consider one of Lucie's dearest friends, so close as to be almost a sister-by-association, marriageable.

She shrugged. "Honestly, the morning when he returned home and caused such a scuffle, I imagined he was absolutely foxed."

It was no secret that young men sometimes drank to excess, with the resulting inebriated state being less than socially acceptable or seemly. Lucie was young, but she was not naïve. She knew drinking often led to ill behavior, and she could not place her own brother so far above the standards of his peers as to believe he was any less capable of over-indulgence than the next fellow.

"Truth to tell, I also wondered the same, that he might be in his cups. I am sorry, I fear that sounds insulting, but it is not how I intend the statement."

Miranda looked chagrined, so Lucie rushed to save her the feeling of further embarrassment.

"Don't be silly. I am perfectly aware of what you meant. I know you would not cast doubts on Oliver's character, nor would you attempt to show him in any less than an admirable light."

Lucie stopped, staring at, but not really seeing, the flamboyant orange-and-white blooms on the bush beside her. She tapped her finger against her lips, carefully choosing her next words.

"Do you think he has some sort of…" She looked around, checking to see whether they were alone. There were no muffled footsteps, no sound of voices and no rustling petticoats so she could only assume their spot amongst the roses was out of sight—and, hopefully, beyond hearing range. "I know it sounds horrid, and I would never venture to speak the notion aloud if I were with someone else, but do you think, perhaps, that Oliver might have gone queer in the attic?"

Miranda's brows lifted so high they nearly disappeared beneath the edge of her artfully arranged curls. She looked so shocked by the suggestion that she almost wished she had not let it pop from her mouth. But she had, and there was no retrieving words after they had escaped one's tongue, so she held her breath and waited, wondering what her companion's response might be.

Thankfully, Miranda had the good sense to speak in a voice just barely above a whisper. She leaned close, and, hardly moving her lips, asked, "Do you think he's touched in the upper works? Like...well...like you-know-who?"

Mentioning George's madness was difficult for anyone devoted to the monarchy. The king's ravings had long since been hidden from public view, but there was not anyone alive who was not aware that the ruler of the country had long ago lost his wits.

"That is precisely what I mean. I am not saying that—heaven forbid!—Oliver is as far gone as, well, you-know-who, but I have begun to wonder whether or not they share the same affliction." Lucie stopped, the reality of her situation hitting her as hard as a load of bricks would have done. She gulped, and then inhaled deeply, filling her lungs with the hope of feeling less restricted and better able to formulate a plan of action. "I don't know what we shall do if it is true, but I do know that"—she lowered her voice to a whisper—"I do know that if my brother has gone crazy we will need to do something about it. We cannot just hide him away, wish him at Jericho, and calmly go about our business. No, something more substantial will have to be done."

As if the matter was settled, the women linked arms and turned themselves around. They strolled more purposefully back to the center of the party, each acting as if they had been busy discussing hemlines instead of mental illness.

Yes, Lucie mused, *something will have to be done. But what? And when?*

More importantly, by whom?

****

Aunt Lucinda waved her over the moment Lucie and Miranda were within waving distance. There was no escaping the demand, so Lucie smiled and dutifully walked toward her sponsor.

The dowager sat on a flowered chaise, low to the ground, padded and comfortable. The young countess had ordered it brought onto the lawn for her mother-in-law's use, and since their arrival from Willowbrook, where Aunt Lucinda had been staying ostensibly to supervise Lucie's social calendar, the elder woman had not moved from the seat. She looked regal in a bold purple frock and matching turban. Amethyst earrings dangled nearly to her shoulders and swayed with every nod of her head.

"Lucinda Jane, where have you been hiding? Why, I have been contemplating sending out a search party for you, my dear." The old woman placed a hand over her heart. "I cannot tell you how I worry about you, or how much my old heart skitters whenever I think of you needing me and my not being close at hand. Oh, perish the thought!"

Her aunt's theatrics were for the benefit of the

gentleman who had been seated on a chair beside her chaise. Upon their arrival, he stood. Now he looked solicitously into the countess's face and said, "Push all ill thoughts from your head, then. Why, your niece and companion are here, and looking fine—and quite lovely. No harm has befallen them, thank God."

He flashed a smile in their direction. Then, he bowed over her aunt and took one of her hands in his. "If I may be so bold, Countess. Would you mind terribly introducing me properly to the ladies? I fear we have not yet met, but that does not mean I do not wish to avail myself of the pleasure of their company."

Sandy blond hair fell in waves nearly to his shoulders, framing a pleasant face whose bright blue eyes were its most remarkable feature. He was tall, almost too tall for Lucie's taste, but well-proportioned, with broad shoulders beneath a crisply-cut white linen shirt. A cravat, the same blue as his eyes, tied around his neck. Tight-fitting knee breeches covered his legs and fit inside polished black Hessian boots.

The effect of his outfit, as well as his casual good looks and boyish charm, was disarming after their walk in the rose garden. Lucie felt like she had gone from nightmare to dream in the beat of a heart, having gone from discussing lunacy to pleasant company in a similar span of time.

"Whatever am I thinking?" Aunt Lucinda waved her free hand toward Lucie, giving her a no-nonsense quirking of one eyebrow to lend credence to the introduction. "Lucinda Jane, I do not believe you have been introduced to a fine gentleman, an especial friend to my dear son, Carson. This, my dear, is Lord Stuart Bailey, the Duke of Chichester. Lord Bailey, this is my niece, Miss Lucinda Jane Gregory, of London and her dear friend, Miss Miranda Spencer, also of London."

The introduction was cordial, almost bland. Both Lucie and Miranda dipped into polite curtsies while the duke bowed.

Lucie murmured, "Your Grace."

Miranda did the same. "Your Grace."

He nodded to each woman in turn. "Miss Gregory. Miss Spencer. It is a delight to meet both of you. Miss Gregory, your aunt was just regaling me with tales of your excellent riding abilities. I must admit, I am impressed with her description of your prowess. I would be honored if someday you might consent to go riding with me." He smiled, and then smoothly turned to include Miranda in the invitation. "Of course, if you also have a fondness for riding, I would very much like to extend the same invitation to you, Miss Spencer."

"Oh, I am sure Lucinda Jane would love that, Stuart. And, by all means, please call her by her Christian name, won't you? It seems too nice a day to stand on pomp and circumstance, doesn't it?"

Her aunt kept her manner casual, but Lucie knew better. This introduction, and subsequent invitation, was the reason she had been so insistent on Lucie's attending the lawn party. Now she saw why no amount of foot-dragging or complaining had gotten her anywhere. She might as well have been speaking to herself or, better yet, to an imaginary cohort. If she had grumbled to some made-up personage, there would have been better odds on her at least having one set of ears which heeded her words.

The duke looked askance at her, so Lucie shrugged and gave him a slight smile. Why fight the unfightable?

Too many battles demanded her attention at present; this one, with its first-name insignificance, did not matter at all.

"Lucinda Jane, then," he said with a rakish grin. "If I may be so bold…it is a fetching name for an equally fetching young lady."

The flattering remark was sweet and brought affection to her heart. Miranda giggled beside her, covering her mouth with one hand while she elbowed Lucie in the side with her other arm. One would have believed the duke had waxed poetic, their response being over-zealous by far for hearing the compliment. Theirs had been a trying afternoon, however, so any nicety was truly welcomed.

Her mood felt lighter than it had all day, so she smiled broadly at the new acquaintance.

"That is kind of you to say. I do hope, Your Grace, that you find 'Lucie' equally appealing, for I fear that no one save my dear Aunt Lucinda calls me 'Lucinda Jane'. Why, I do not believe I would even respond to a call by that name if I did not hear my aunt's voice."

He turned toward the dowager, one brow raised in question. "Is this true? Does your namesake respond only to the abbreviated version of your elegant moniker?"

Color flooded the elderly woman's face, turning her cheeks a shade of pink usually reserved for the finest rose blooms. She smiled so broadly her cheeks folded into wrinkles, and said, "It is the God's honest truth, I am afraid. Nowadays young women are less formal than the older generation, less inclined to maintain some semblance of rigidity. So Lucinda Jane is shortened by everyone except me. Even her parents use the girlish nickname. I will never call my niece anything other than the name she was baptized with, the same one that has been suitable for my use all these years. You, sir, may do as you please—that is, as long as what pleases you also pleases me."

The implication was clear. He could call Lucie by the nickname, but he ought to not even dream of taking any further liberties. Protocol and social rigors must be maintained, despite the business of name-shortening.

The duke bowed his head. "I understand completely." Then he turned to face Lucie. "I wonder if you would consent to take a short drive. I have asked permission from your sponsor, and she has kindly given it, so if you are amenable to the venture…" He stopped, and then gazed into Miranda's eyes. "Of course, I wish to include you in the invitation, Miss Spencer. That is, if your chaperone can be located so I may obtain permission to whisk you away."

Aunt Lucinda cut into the conversation. She gave a gasp of surprise, as if she had just recalled the other's presence. "Oh, Miranda my dear, I am so sorry. I completely forgot to tell you—your sister Amy is searching for you. She and that nice young man, Lyle— oh, what is his name again?" The elderly woman snapped her fingers, looking completely vexed, searching in vain to grasp the name from memory. Before either Miranda or Lucie could supply the man's last name, Aunt Lucinda waved her hand in the air beside her head, pushing the notion away. "Never mind, it doesn't matter. I am sure you know of whom I speak. Anyhow, Amy and her gentleman have recently been hunting for you. Something about a dinner invitation at your neighbor's home, I believe. The last I saw of them, they were making their way to the main house. I told Amy I would send you after her when I saw you next."

Miranda's expression left no room for ambiguity. She was crestfallen, and Lucie felt sorry for her. Had it been possible, Lucie would have gladly traded places with her. It was obvious her friend wanted to go for a ride with the duke much more than she did.

"Thank you, ma'am. I am sorry I cannot accompany you, Your Grace. I am sure that you and Lucie will have a fine time. If you will excuse me, then." With a final curtsey and a fast hug for Lucie, she turned away and began the short walk up to the main house.

Lucie watched her go with longing in her heart. She felt at the mercy of her situation, completely unable to formulate her own plans, keep her own schedule or air her views without Aunt Lucinda's jumping in to correct her. At least with someone by her side, she had an ally. Now she was on her own—again.

"So." The duke rubbed his hands together, smiling down at her from his impressive height. "It seems only you and I remain. Would you favor me by riding around the lane? I must tell you, my horses are fleet-footed and the sporty curricle I have recently purchased makes one feel borne on the wings of angels. Are you up to the excitement, and challenge, of riding with me?"

She said the first thing that popped into her head. "I promise you, I am up to far greater challenges than even riding in an angel-borne curricle can provide."

Chapter 4

Lucie shuddered, wrapping her arms around her middle to comfort herself. Unfortunately, no amount of hugging could calm her frayed nerves.

What on earth could possibly be keeping Doctor Fairwater in Father's room so long?

Perhaps he is just taking his time with the process. Being extra-careful, and checking everything twice, the way Father Christmas does with his list of good and naughty children.

The image brought a small smile to her lips, but it did not reach her eyes or warm her heart. Nothing could—or would—warm her frightened, frigid heart until she heard that her father was going to be all right.

It was almost inconceivable that just yesterday afternoon she and Stuart had been trotting around the Waltham estate. Wind had blown their hair into their eyes, laughter had come easily over the most insignificant trifles, and the feeling of exhilaration and freedom she had experienced being jostled about in the two-person conveyance had lifted the gloomy mantle from her shoulders. She had felt alive, and almost happy, in a way she had not since Oliver's arrival at Willowbrook Manor.

Now, the feeling was completely gone, a memory that felt like it belonged to someone else. Surely she could not be the same light-hearted, carefree woman who had shared a few hours of pleasant company with a solicitous suitor?

No, that could not be—*was* not, for sure—the same woman who now walked the floor outside Father's room. Lucie's footsteps fell silently, their force lost to the deep pile of the hand-loomed runner that stretched the length of the hallway. She was glad she was not causing a disturbance, grateful that she was not adding to her father's discomfort.

Memories of the day tumbled through her mind like small stones caught in the rushing water of a rain-flooded stream.

He seemed fine at breakfast. Perfectly normal, and healthy. His color was good. His cheeks—rosy and his eyes bright. Oh, good Lord, what happened?

How had he gone from healthy to bed-ridden in such short order? It made no sense at all.

Of course, Lord Gregory had been under the weather for quite some time, but nothing in his past episodes of feeling poorly was anything near as distressing as this. Before he had looked peaked, tired more rapidly than he had in his younger days, and retired earlier in the evening. He was, after all, getting on in years, so much of his physical decline was attributed to age rather than infirmity.

Still, the doctor had warned them of his "vapors" and had advised a regiment of light fare, prolonged rest, and activities which relaxed the mind while refreshing the body. Had they not paid attention enough to his prescription for renewed health? Had they—

Oh, I cannot stand this waiting! How long can they be? Why doesn't someone poke their head out of the room and at least let me know he is alive? Is that too much to ask?

Lucie's hands curled into fists. Her fingernails bit mercilessly into the soft, fleshy pads of her palms but she did not flinch. Any pain she could inflict upon herself, any discomfort at all might take some of Father's suffering from him. If there was a God in heaven—and she devoutly believed there was—it was only just that she take some of her family's pain, and share the burden. It was willingly, and deliberately, done.

With a stifled groan of frustration, Lucie tightened her fingers. How much more could she take without losing her mind? If the door to Father's room did not open before the grandfather clock at the end of the hall chimed again, she was going to knock and ask to be granted entrance.

She paced, praying quietly as she did so, for nearly twenty minutes more, and had made up her mind to rap lightly on Father's doorframe when, to her enormous relief, the door opened. Doctor Fairwater emerged, looking too serious by far. He had cared for Lucie since the day of her birth, nursing her through childhood illnesses, a broken arm, and the assorted afflictions that anyone might encounter. Their long association had given her an insight into the man's character, and a distinct feel for reading his moods. What she saw now on the face of their plump, middle-aged physician did not make her happy, or instill confidence. He looked worried, and she rushed to his side as he closed the door behind him.

"Please, Doctor, tell me Father is fine. Please, I beg you, tell me he is going to get well."

The words caught in her throat, and she gasped as

the tears she had been holding at bay finally fell over the rims of her eyes and down her cheeks. Her mint green morning dress had been donned with great expectations for the day ahead. Now it was forgotten, merely a convenient rag with which to soak up her tears as they fell from her face.

Doctor Fairwater put an arm about her shoulders, and pulled her close against his side. The scent of his pipe tobacco filled her head, comforting in its familiarity. He gave her an affectionate squeeze and led her down the long hallway.

Every step they took from Father's room frightened Lucie. She felt, irrationally, she knew, that her nearness might bolster his strength. She fully believed that by remaining close to the one man who had loved her unconditionally her entire life, she might keep him safer than he might be if she were not near. In her heart, she felt her closeness might force his heart to beat, and air to flow in and out of his lungs, until his body healed and he required her strength no longer.

Sometimes childish viewpoints carry on into adulthood, especially when those beliefs have long-established roots that dig deep into one's heart.

"My dear, you must not fret so."

He did not answer her questions. He did not rush to reassure her that Father would, indeed, recover. The doctor did not even pass a comment on the man's condition, deflecting instead all attention from the patient and onto her.

A chill, its icy fingers intrusive and penetrating, crept into her chest.

Good God in heaven, he must be worse than I think he is.

With that dire thought in her mind, she planted her feet on the costly rug and refused to take one more step. The physician was forced to stop, although he attempted to move her a few steps further. With a small *tut-tut*, he turned to face her. In the doctor's eyes she saw much of what she feared. Not only was her father not well, the illness afflicting him was of a more serious nature than Lucie had even allowed herself to consider.

For the first time in her life, she stood for a moment and contemplated her father's death. Had she eaten anything at all she was certain to have cast up her accounts, but thankfully, she had not so much as touched her breakfast before Father took ill.

Doctor Fairwater took a large pocket handkerchief from his vest pocket. Wordlessly he wiped her cheeks, and then handed the fabric to her.

"Blow your nose. Then we shall go into the study and talk."

Dutifully she blew her nose. She nodded, and then remembered her manners. Her mother was still in Father's room so the duty of playing hostess at the manor fell to her. She took a deep breath, squared her shoulders, and led the way to the study.

"I shall ring for tea to be brought in at once, Doctor. You must be famished."

****

Three hours after Doctor Fairwater had gone, Lucie was still in the study.

She had not left the room, not even when Elaine, one of the downstairs maids, had come to ask where she intended to take her midday meal. The answer had been clear-cut. She did not intend to eat, not at midday or anytime in the foreseeable future. Food, and life in general, had lost its appeal. She had no appetite—for anything or anyone.

She stared doggedly at the floor-to-ceiling bookcases that ran wall-to-wall around the room. They made the vast space feel less imposing and cavernous, more inviting and far cozier by far than it should have been given its height and width. The leather-bound volumes provided no answers to the dilemma afflicting her mind. Lucie had read a great many of them, some several times over, but even with all their knowledge they gave her no solutions.

Botheration! How could a life that seemed so simple, so effortless and charmed, fall into such an abysmal state in such short order? Just days earlier all she had to consider was the color of her slippers, the fullness of her dance card, or the beading on a reticule. Now the whole Gregory clan had fallen under the horses' hooves and was in imminent danger of becoming trampled.

What to do if something happens to Father? Oliver is…oh, no. Who knows what Oliver is?

She slapped her hand on the polished mahogany surface of the desktop in front of her. Her skin stung, but she was so upset she smacked her hand—hard—on the wood a second time. Now she curled her fingers and pulled her hand protectively against her chest. It hurt, just like she did. There was so much pain coursing through her mind that the tingling palm paled by comparison.

She had kicked off her shoes hours earlier and placed her feet in a very un-ladylike position on the desktop. Her toes pushed aside the wide leather blotter, and her legs crossed at the ankles. A fair view of her stockinged calf was on display, but as she was very much alone, there was no one to see it. No one to be scandalized.

If she did not figure a way out of their current situation, being the focus of a scandal would be the least of her worries.

The doctor's parting words rang in Lucie's head like church bells stuck on the same note, sounding over and over until the person hearing them either went mad or plugged their ears with cotton. Since the words were inside her head, even huge wads of cotton would not help her.

Doctor Fairwater did not attempt to blow sunshine in her face or hide the truth. His words were spoken somberly, in a tone of voice she had never before heard him use. "He needs to rest. If he does not do so, I fear the worst."

Fear the worst...fear the worst...fear the—

"I came as soon as I heard!" Miranda's entrance, uncharacteristically exuberant and with enough force that when she pushed open the heavy door she did so with such strength that it hammered against the wood-paneled wall behind it. The noise stopped her in her tracks, but only temporarily. With a rushed apology, she continued into the room, stopping short on the other side of the wide desk. She appeared indecisive, and it occurred to Lucie her good friend had a mind to leap across the desk to grab her in a comforting embrace.

She held up her hand, bringing Miranda to a halt before she could take another step.

Elaine appeared at the door, and looked questioningly at her employer. Lucie smiled, showing all was well—albeit noisy. "We are fine, Elaine. Please inform the cook that we would like a tea tray sent in here post haste." She turned a speculative eye on Miranda, and then added, "Please be sure there are some scones—orange scones—on the tray as well. That will be all."

"Certainly, miss." The maid curtsied before she left. She closed the door softly behind her, leaving the two women to stare at each other for several heartbeats.

Lucie could not think of one thing to say, so she gestured toward the low, comfortable brown leather chair situated directly behind Miranda. Miranda sat, and then they contemplated each other for several seconds more.

They had never been shy with each other before, so this not knowing how to begin or what to say felt strange. But then, they had never discussed a grave illness with regard to one of their parents before, either. The territory was new and uncharted...and somewhat fear-provoking.

Being an adult was one thing. Assuming accountability for an entire family, and the household, was another prospect entirely. Lucie was utterly unprepared for the event. She felt suddenly years older than her dearest friend. The weight of her situation had somehow stolen all carefree notions or small freedoms she may have had at her disposal. Now she felt entirely responsible—whether she wanted to or not.

The first thing—and it was a small thing, really—Lucie thought to do was smile.

Miranda exhaled, a long sigh of relief that showed she had been holding her breath since she spoke her last word. She smiled in return, fanning her red cheeks with one gloved hand.

"I have been running ever since I heard your father was struck down. One of our downstairs maids spread the word to Jenny. Of course Jenny has been my maid for so long she knows what a fond closeness you and I share, so she brought the news above stairs along with my breakfast tray."

Leave it to the servants to spread the news of Lord Gregory's illness. Theirs was a more reliable source of information than *The London Daily Gazette*. More expedient, as well.

Leaning forward with a brisk shake of her head, Miranda hurried to add, "I didn't eat my breakfast, mind you. Not one teeny, tiny bite—not once I heard the news. Jenny dressed me while the carriage was brought around, and then I ran out of the house and over here like a woman possessed."

A tendency to lean toward chubbiness had been the bane of Miranda's existence since she was a toddler with a sugar biscuit clutched in each hand. Now that she had gained maturity she had slimmed down, but she had never lost her fondness for good food or sweets. It spoke volumes about her current state, knowing she had run from a fully loaded, and probably exceedingly tempting, breakfast tray.

Lucie appreciated the sacrifice.

"Thank you for coming." She meant it, too. These past hours she had needed privacy and quiet, so that she could think without distractions. But she had pondered so long and hard her head ached. It was a welcome relief to see Miranda, and she was grateful for the company.

"He's not...um, your father, did he...?" Miranda paled and looked like she might vomit on the spot, so

Lucie shook her head.

There had been no time to dress her hair this morning, so it still hung in a thick braid, lying like a sleeping brown snake down the right side of her chest. She still would have been in her nightdress, had she not been in the habit of donning her clothes before allowing her hair to be done up. Now she tossed the braid over her shoulder, its weight light by comparison to the multitude of other items her slim shoulders carried at present.

"No, father is not dead." Lucie said a silent prayer of thanks that he was still with them, hopefully resting well in his room upstairs. "He gave us a fright, but he…well, he did not give up the ghost."

"Thank God." Miranda scrubbed a single tear from her cheek. It was no secret that both she and Amy held Lord Gregory in higher esteem than they did their own father. They saw Lucie's parents more frequently than they did their own, and the Gregory parents took greater interest in them than theirs ever had. "For a dreadful minute I feared he might have…you know."

Lucie was touched Miranda could not bring herself to say the words. She nodded, feeling her own throat tighten.

If she did not take control of the conversation, it would not be long before they were both sobbing, so she took a deep breath and put all ideas of death from her head.

"I know, dear, but he didn't, so we must not dwell on that. Do not even let the idea into your head—lest it somehow grow a life of its own, escape and come true. I will endeavor to do the same." She smiled brightly, showing that she was already making the effort to do so. "Is that a deal? Can I count on you to put only good thoughts into your consciousness where Father is concerned?"

"You can." Miranda's eyes were bright. "Only good, positive thoughts."

A tap at the door announced the tea. They waited until the tray had been set on a corner of the desk and the maid had left them alone in the room once again.

Lucie poured a cup, setting it down in front of her friend. She pushed the milk and sugar closer to Miranda before she poured herself a cup of tea. Taking the beverage black, she sat back against the comfortable chair and took a sip. The liquid was hot and soothing.

She watched while Miranda helped herself to a scone, buttered it, and took a large bite. Lucie waited until the scone was eaten and her own tea cup was empty before she spoke.

"Father is very ill."

How to broach the myriad of issues swimming like frantic fish through her brain? At the beginning, she realized in a burst of clarity. The way out of the family's dilemma surely had to be taken one baby step at a time, and in a logical order—didn't it?

"I felt as much." Miranda seemed hesitant to push too hard for information, although desire for it was written all over her pretty face. "So…"

Now that the time had come, the admission came hard.

She was, however, compelled to go on. "Right. Yes, well, Father is gravely ill, as a matter of fact. It is…it is…well, it appears his condition is quite grim, I am afraid."

"Did the doctor say what is wrong with him?"

"He did." She had not said the words aloud yet. Saying them somehow made the situation feel truer than it did when the words were held back by her teeth and tongue. She had to say them sooner or later, and she supposed the first person she told should be someone she loved and trusted like a member of the family. It was, after all, a family affair.

Taking a moment to fortify herself, Lucie paused. Then, she said sadly, "It is his heart. Apparently he has had palpitations for some time now, and he and Mother, as well as Doctor Fairwater, have been concealing the fact."

"You cannot be serious."

Shock painted Miranda's face pink, her mouth formed an "o" and her eyes opened so widely that had they not been discussing a matter of life-or-death she would have looked comical. But they were, so she was not funny at all.

Lucie shrugged her shoulders. Tension made the motion painful. She had not been aware of just how exceedingly tight her muscles had become these past hours. Her jaw hurt, her temple throbbed and the headache that had threatened to arrive hit her hard.

"I am, unfortunately, dreadfully serious. You know he has been under doctor's care for some time now, ostensibly for a case of the 'vapors', right? Well, the vaporous affliction was evidently a cover-up, a concealment to keep the true nature of his health hidden."

She could hardly believe it herself that her parents had been in cahoots and kept such vital information secret. The fact was offensive and would have normally turned her temper up a notch but now, with everything weighing so heavily on her, she could not find the energy to take offense. Perhaps later, when Father and Oliver were both well again and life at Willowbrook Manor returned to some semblance of normal, she might have a word—or two or three—with her parents just to let them know how hurt she was at being kept in the dark about something so key to their well-being. Now, however, was not the time.

"Oh, Lucie, I am so sorry." Miranda's hand flew to her chest, covering her heart. "I knew something was wrong with him, but I never supposed it was so significant. Is there...oh, please tell me there is something that can be done. Something to make him stronger, or to cure him—please, say it is so!"

Inhaling, and then exhaling, with careful deliberation gave Lucie time to consider her reply. She nodded.

"Yes, there is much that can be done to build Father up. First, he must not have any nervous tension in his life. The doctor says that any strain or undue worry may bring on more heart palpitations. Each episode may be the last one, I am afraid, so stress of any nature is entirely off-limits."

How to allay Father's stress given the current household climate? That was the difficulty—and it was all hers, for there was no one to share the burden, not even kind-hearted Miranda. No, figuring out how to keep her father alive and Willowbrook under control was Lucie's predicament—hers, and hers alone.

Her thoughts distilled until a single mantra remained, obliterating every lingering doubt she harbored, each niggling shred of fear that had insinuated itself into her psyche.

Father will live...Father will live...Father will live...

Chapter 5

Any thrill Lucie might have ordinarily experienced at the prospect of an evening at Almack's was not as great as it normally would have been, had the timing been different. The most exclusive assembly rooms in London and the pinnacle of dreams for every woman who aspired to be *someone* someday—even if she was *no one* at present—required a pass from one of the patroness' of the place in order to venture one toe past the hallowed front door. Lucie had obtained a pass, courtesy of Aunt Lucinda who personally, and on very close terms, knew Lady Sefton.

Lucie had the entrée but not the heart for the occasion. Still, a pass for Almack's could not be disregarded just because it came at an inconvenient time in one's life.

Smoothing a gloved hand down the front of her skirt, Lucie resolved to make the most of the evening. Dressed as she was, in a gown created specifically for her and designed to show her figure at its best, would be wasteful if she did not attempt to feel pleased with her present state of affairs.

Tomorrow she could go back to dealing with the obligations of her family situation. This night, however, seemed suited for magic—even if she did drag her slippered feet.

Why ruin a perfectly beautiful pair of slippers? I

*shall try to enjoy myself—minimally, of course. I must
not be too exuberant in my merry-making, not with
things at home such a bumblebroth.*

Aunt Lucinda's seamstress had outdone herself on
the creation Lucie wore. With an empire waist, low-cut,
yet demure and tasteful neckline and short tulip sleeves,
the pale yellow silk showed off her green eyes and
russet brown hair to her best advantage. The gown's
underskirt, also expensive imported silk, was a shade
lighter than the body of the dress and gave fluidity to
the fabrics that was more illusionary than actual. The
effect was mesmerizing, and magical, and Lucie adored
the ensemble.

She would have been happier had the situation at
Willowbrook Manor had not existed. Knowing
something was amiss within the family buzzed at her
mercilessly, like a persistent mosquito torturing all of
her waking moments. The Gregory state of affairs even
haunted her dreams, turning her usually restful
nocturnal hours into times filled with heartless
nightmares.

"Smile, my dear. You look like you are about to
enter into a Smithfield Bargain of the foulest, most
despicable degree." Her aunt tilted her head to one side,
mutely examining Lucie's face while she tapped the tip
of one gloved finger against the side of her nose. Lucie
noted the face powder residue smeared on the glove tip
when Aunt Lucinda held up her finger in front of her
face, as if she had just had the brightest idea of her long
life. "No! I have it! Your sour expression reminds me
of a woman dangling after a confirmed bachelor." She
stopped, sucked in a fast breath, and then asked in a low
tone of voice, so low that no one else could hear, "You

aren't, are you? You haven't set your sights on someone entirely unsuitable, have you, my dear niece?"

Lucie rushed to reassure her. "No, I haven't. Honestly, Aunt Lucinda, you can be quite vexing at times. You know very well the situation at home. How in the world could I possibly concentrate on romance, or setting my sights on anyone, right now? It is—oh! It is absolutely unthinkable."

With a wave of her hand, Aunt Lucinda dismissed the protestation. She smiled sagely, as if she had been expecting Lucie's declaration.

"Pish posh! It is never—I repeat, *never*—unthinkable to contemplate romance, my dear."

Lucie cast a dubious look at the proclamation and Aunt Lucinda sighed. The sound seemed pulled from her toes, and the feel of it pushed all the gaiety of their surroundings down to mere background noise. Lucie's attention, every particle of it, focused on her aunt.

Never before had Lucie seen such a girlish, animated expression in Aunt Lucinda's eyes. It almost made her wonder whether the aged woman had taken herself on a journey back in time, remembering her days and nights of laughter and parties, of ball gowns and dance cards. If so, Lucie was along for the trip, and she vowed not to miss a moment of the adventure.

A circle of light, cast by the flickering glow of the candlelight shining from the wall sconce above their heads, shut them off from the rest of the party. They were insulated, separated from everyone and everything else by the shared reminiscences of the dowager countess.

Lucie held her breath, and waited for her aunt to continue.

Aunt Lucinda did not disappoint, nor did she hold back the flood of memories the enchantment of the night had unleashed.

With a firm grip, the dowager grasped Lucie's hand and tugged her close. They were nearly nose to nose, their heads bent so close the ostrich feather in Aunt Lucinda's headdress danced an inch above Lucie's piled curls.

The invitation to share confidences was just as wonderful, if not better than, the foray into Almack's. The night was a passing event, but secrets could warm a heart for a lifetime.

"I know you believe me to be an old woman, my dear. That is, sadly, true now but, I am glad to say, it was not always the case. Oh, not that I mind getting on in years. Age gives one latitude to press the boundaries of social convention and…and other things as well. Let's leave it at that, shan't we?"

Lucie knew better than to interrupt her aunt's reflective attitude. She produced a tiny grin, and the slightest nod of her head. It was all that was required of her, so it was all she gave.

"As I was saying, my dear…"

The older woman paused, and fear that the tale would end before it began gripped her, but she need not have worried. Aunt Lucinda was in full steam.

Shaking her head as if to clear cobwebs, Aunt Lucinda went on. Her voice had taken a girlish tenor and, when Lucie stared deeply into the watery gray eyes she knew so well, she could see the younger version of her aunt. It was, she realized with staggering transparency, a slightly—*very* slightly—older version of herself that she saw mirrored in the eyes of her sponsor.

"Well, as I was trying to tell you—to *impress upon you* most vehemently, my dear—it is never the wrong time to contemplate romance. I will swear on a stack of Bibles, it is one of the truest truths I have uncovered in all my years on this earth. Love and romance…they are well worth entertaining at any time, and in any circumstance."

There was a message in her aunt's words, Lucie knew that as well as she knew her own name, but the significance had not yet made itself known to her. She concentrated on finding the hidden meaning behind Aunt Lucinda's words. Suddenly it was more important by far than anything else around her.

Fortunately, Aunt Lucinda had more to say. Much more.

"I am going to let you in on a little secret, one I hadn't meant to share with you until further along in the Season, until after you took a shine to a special young man. But, circumstances being what they are, I feel you might need a small lift."

Aunt Lucinda gazed searchingly into Lucie's eyes. For a heartbeat she felt as uncovered and exposed as a newborn babe. It was as if her aunt innocently plumbed the depths of her heart. When the older woman smiled knowingly, Lucie released a pent-up breath. She had passed whatever test it was that had been given.

"Yes, just as I thought…a bit of a chin-lifter is in order, my dear. So, the advice I have kept close to my bosom all these long, long years." The dowager countess crossed her arms tightly across her chest, hugging her memories close one last time before sharing them. She gave a quick, almost imperceptible, nod, as if reassuring herself that this was, indeed, the right time to divulge her secrets.

"Lucinda Jane, you are my namesake, and as such I know I can trust you with what I have held dearest my entire lifetime. It may not mean much, or help you find your way out of the current, sad predicament you are in, but then again, it just may…yes, it just may at that. So, before I begin what will, I confess, be a shorter story than its prologue has been, I want to make certain that your mind is at ease this moment over your father's state of health. He is, this very hour, resting contentedly with your mother. You know that, don't you?"

It was the truth. The Gregorys were comfortably ensconced in the library when Lucie and Aunt Lucinda had left for Almack's. Father looked hale, if not somewhat hearty, and had not suffered another irregular beating of his heart since the last attack, two days prior.

Lucie had no doubt her parents would read for hours, and then retire to their rooms for the night. It was their habit, one long ingrained and hardly ever deviated from.

"Yes, I do. Father looked well when we left, and I have no fear he is fine."

"Good. Now that we have got that out of the way, I will tell you all I know about love, life and romance."

At last! The heart of the matter.

Her demeanor so serious and her voice so hushed it might have been the secrets of the realm that were being imparted in the assembly room rather than the beliefs of an aged woman, Aunt Lucinda placed her mouth beside Lucie's ear. Tiny wisps of air stirred the ringlets that had been so artfully arranged, and the combination of breath and stirring hair tickled Lucie so completely she barely held a giggle in check.

"The heart knows, my dear."

The heart knows? That was it—the secret to end all secrets, the morsel to quench her distress?

The heart knows? Lucie could barely believe her own ears!

"Pardon?" Lucie's brow furrowed. She puzzled over the statement but could not make sense of it.

Aunt Lucinda leaned back, rested her spine against the brocade-covered wall behind her, and smiled so complacently it seemed rude to push her further. But the matter could not drop, regardless of the smugness of the smile or the obvious satisfaction her aunt felt. Lucie would not—*could* not—walk away from the conversation before she understood entirely the point being made.

When her aunt refused to say more, Lucie considered shaking the logic behind the statement out of her. She was not ordinarily prone to fits of physicality, although she had been pushed to contemplate them twice this week. While she had not needed to resort to face slapping to calm Miranda down, Lucie had no doubt she could conjure at the very minimum a teensy, tiny wobbling of her aunt's shoulders beneath her own gloved hands.

The heart knows? It must be some kind of trick, some sort of Almack's prank the older women played on the younger set. What else could it be?

Still…

Aunt Lucinda looked as satisfied as the Sphinx—and just as silent. Her lips formed a tight smile, and without being told Lucie knew she would get no more from the woman—not even if she were to attempt to shake her. This, of course, had been only a passing thought, one which would never, ever become reality.

Lucie sighed, and then, remembering her etiquette, said, "I shall commit to memory that bit of information, Aunt. All of my days, I will keep the notion close at…uh, close at heart. Thank you for sharing."

"Certainly, my dear." Then, looking pointedly over Lucie's shoulder, the dowager said, "Good evening. How pleasant to see you again."

"The pleasure is all mine, ma'am."

That voice. That glorious, heart-stopping voice.

Awareness shot through Lucie like a bolt of summer lightning. It was hot, and fast, and made her toes curl inside her ivory doeskin dancing slippers.

No other man had the same effect on her; it was both disconcerting and exhilarating, and she hardly knew how to arrange her features before she turned to face him. After a half-second of consideration, she decided to allow her expression to govern itself, and brought what she hoped was a neutral smile to her lips.

She turned. The duke stood a scant two feet away. Had she whirled more quickly, or been less sure-footed, she might have tumbled into his arms. But she did not, and her footing inside the handmade slippers was as comfortable as if she had been barefoot, so her turn was graceful.

Routinely Lucie dipped into a curtsey. "Lord Grayson."

He inclined his head. Then he did the most astonishing thing and caught Lucie completely off guard. The duke stretched out his right arm, took her gloved hand in his, and brought it to his lips. The kiss he placed on her knuckles was fleeting, but when he released her fingertips from his grasp, the memory of his touch lingered.

"Miss Gregory. It is a pleasure to see you again."

"And you as well."

He looked incredible in his evening clothes—so dashing, in fact, that Lucie could hardly keep her gaze from sweeping down, then up—then down to his toes again. An elegant evening coat in the darkest coal gray she had ever seen coordinated flawlessly with a vest the same shade and gray pinstripe trousers that were so immaculately pressed their pleats looked able to slice through a loaf of bread.

A starched white shirt provided the background for an expertly tied cravat. It was the only item which provided a splash of color to his ensemble. Lord Grayson's cravat was almost the exact same shade of pale yellow as her gown.

He looked self-assured and wealthy, a man who knew his mind and was aware of the impact he made on his surroundings. There was an almost awe-inspiring presence to him, and Lucie wondered if everyone could sense it or if it was only she who was thusly affected.

Because she *was* affected by the man; there was no rejecting the notion.

To her utter delight, it appeared the duke was somewhat influenced by her presence, as well. He stared into her eyes for a long moment, almost too long to be deemed proper, as if he sought something known only to him.

"If you might permit me a somewhat forward observation…" He smiled, reminding her without a word that he was, by far, the handsomest man she had gazed upon—or whose gaze had touched her so thoroughly. "You look exquisite tonight, Miss Gregory. You far outshine all others in the room…that is, if any man were able to notice the others when presented with a woman as charming as yourself. Which, I hasten to assure you, I have not—noticed anyone else, that is."

Her tongue felt glued to the top of her mouth. Had her ears deceived her? Had he really said what she thought he said, or were the words only figments of her over-tired imagination?

Lord Grayson smiled, as if he murmured flattery of such magnitude daily. "Although I am aware of perhaps being considered a tad too forward, I am not a man who plays games easily. I have, much to my dear, demure grandmother's embarrassment, a knack for telling the truth when I might keep my mouth closed instead. It is a talent that sometimes lands me in the soup, but leaves no room for error about my feelings or intentions."

He smiled again, and Lucie felt the candlelight dim by comparison. She said nothing, and merely waited for him to continue. The conversation, even though it was pointedly one-sided at this juncture, was by far the most fascinating of her life. She held her breath, and wondered what the duke would say next.

Leaning forward a bit, so close she caught a whiff of his cologne and saw the smoothness of his freshly shaven cheeks, he said, "I have no stomach for falsehood or fabrication. It is only fair, I believe, that I inform you of that defect in my character at the earliest opportunity. Some cannot stand a man who does not wax poetic when his heart is not behind the words. It is, I suppose, a personal predilection. So, that is the bare fact; I dislike dishonesty and deceit, and will not tolerate them in my life. Nor will I put up with those qualities from anyone I deal with." He stopped, studied her for a minute, and then asked, "How do you feel about my confession?"

Lucie's head spun. Since she had come out, she had met many men, each with a unique style and some with more idiosyncrasies than others. She had never met one who made such a proclamation so early on in their acquaintance.

No, that was not true. She had never met any man who had *ever* made such a strong statement about anything—at *any* point in their acquaintance.

It was refreshing. It was unnerving. It left her speechless, but he waited for her response. Lucie had the feeling Lord Grayson might wait until the day after forever if he had to do so.

"I, ah, completely agree." Dishonesty was not something she admired or a practice she engaged in, so why not tell the truth about…well, about the truth? It made sense, if only in a convoluted way.

The duke looked even more dashing when he laughed, which he did now. His gaze danced over her face, bringing heat to her cheeks.

"I am glad—*very glad*—to hear that, Miss Gregory." He paused, and then held out his arm. "Would you do me the honor of taking a turn about the room? I would love the opportunity to get to know you better, and I believe we might find we share some common interests. So, what do you say?"

She did not hesitate, but slipped her arm through his and rested her hand lightly on the duke's forearm. They fell into step effortlessly, as if they had been walking side by side together for ages rather than minutes.

At first, they discussed the weather.

Then, a brief chat about books. When asked her favorite author, Lucie named Homer.

The duke looked astonished by the admission and pressed her about her choice. He seemed about to contest the point until she admitted the reason she enjoyed the ancient writer was because his epics were character-driven and focused on the journey of the man, rather than the plight of the outside world. She cited *The Odyssey* as an example of victory against all odds that could be applied to any era. Lord Grayson contemplated for a few strides, and she imagined he might offer resistance but he did not even raise a word to dispute her assertion.

With a nod of overt satisfaction, the duke said, "Very well said, Miss Gregory. I see you are a woman whose intelligence is as delightful as her beauty. I am impressed, very much so, with your acute insight. I shall look upon Homer with new eyes when I read him next, thank you."

"My pleasure."

There was no accusation that she was more bluestocking than was fashionable, and Lucie was relieved. She had spoken without contemplating the ramifications. After all, they were at Almack's where the focus of the evening was primarily impressing, and being impressed by, the most eligible of polite society. It was not the time for intellectual discussions, but, thankfully, the duke did not seem to mind.

She was surprised when, after another turn around the room, Lord Grayson enquired about her father's health. How could he know Lord Gregory was ill? It had only been days since he had been stricken, and there had been no public, or formal, mention of the man's state.

"My father?" Lucie looked intently into the dark eyes of the man beside her, searching for clues regarding his inside knowledge. "How on earth do you know my father has taken ill? It is not something we have discussed outside the walls of Willowbrook Manor. I must admit, I am flummoxed by your having such intimate knowledge of our family's goings-on. Pray tell, how do you come by such news?"

Lord Grayson shrugged, his broad shoulders stretching his evening jacket tight across the muscular form it concealed. She felt the power in the man. It sent a tiny tingle of excitement dancing across her skin but she was too intently waiting for his reply to pay much attention to her own feelings.

He made no attempt to hide the source of his intelligence. "I fear we are subject to what I like to call 'the servants' information service'."

Understanding dawned. *Of course, the servants!*

"Ah, I understand now. It was the servants who spread the word."

Lucie shook her head in amazement, and a lock of hair fell across her cheek. It was part of one of the curls beside her right ear. Had Aunt Lucinda been beside her, Lucie would have been chastised for shaking her head too enthusiastically. It was not, she had been told countless times, proper to present oneself in a mussed state in public.

She was about to reach up to pat the lock into place when Lord Grayson performed the move. No man had touched her so before, and the gesture made her forget her surprise over his having known about life inside

Willowbrook Manor.

Her breath caught in her throat. The thumping in her heart was so loud she wondered if Lord Grayson could hear it, or if the pounding was only known to her.

"So soft and silky," he murmured as he tucked the curl into position. "Just as I knew it would be."

She struggled to find a reply. There seemed to be none, so she remained silent.

As he pulled his hand back, Lord Grayson cleared his throat. The sound was deep and masculine, and so markedly different from the dear tone he had used to make his last statement that it brought the moment back into focus with startling clarity.

Lucie decided to ignore Lord Grayson's touch, as well as his assessment of her hair. She was tongue-tied, so any remark she might utter was sure to sound ridiculous. Her mind scrambled for something to say.

Father—talk about Father. Good Lord, talk about anything...just say something!

"My father—"

"Your father—"

Their words collided. They stopped speaking, and halted their stroll, turning to face each other with mutual dumbfounded expressions on their faces. A slight pause, then laughter! Every ounce of tension between them vanished, borne on the tinkles of their mirth.

After a moment, Lord Grayson put a proprietary hand over hers where it lay on his arm, and began to walk again. The room had grown crowded, but he avoided the other bodies with polite ease. Lucie felt the way she had when they had danced the cotillion. Moving beside the strong, polished man was like floating.

"So," he began after they had taken a few steps, "Lord Gregory is unwell?"

"Unfortunately that is the case." Her heart ached at the memory of her father's illness.

"I am most distressed to hear it. He is a distinguished gentleman, and one of my favorite people." When she looked up in surprise, he smiled and said, "I have had the very distinct—and pleasurable—honor of riding with your father on several occasions. We have been at the same fox hunts, and I have been fortunate enough to discuss politics, literature, and sporting affairs with him. We have, I will allow, shared a few snifters of brandy beside the fire and have had spirited discussions about a surprising number of topics. He is a fine man, and I fervently hope he recovers in due haste."

Lucie could not have been more astounded if Lord Gregory had said he had gone riding with the Queen herself.

How could it be possible that this man was so closely acquainted with her father, and yet she was unaware of it? It seemed impossible, but she knew it was a fact. She saw the sincerity in the duke's eyes when he spoke and knew his assertion that he did not speak anything but the truth was genuine.

He cast a sincere gaze and said, "Please give your father my best wishes. Tell him, if you will, that I would like to call on him when he feels up to receiving company. It has been far too long between visits. And if Lord Grayson is not quite up to sharing a brandy beside the fire, perhaps we might take a cup of tea. I have heard chamomile in an old-fashioned, serviceable

Brown Betty is the thing for chasing an ailment to the devil. I am willing to give it a try, if he is."

Astounding! The man knew Homer, sports, politics...he could flatter more succinctly than any other, and danced like a dream... Now he proved he had a talent for discussing teas, as well.

What else is there to know about you, Lord Grayson? What other secrets and talents do you keep hidden behind those dark eyes of yours?

Chapter 6

Lucie had read the letter so many times the paper was soft, and creased, from being handled so often. The words were committed to memory, but she could not resist opening the missive and reading his sentiments again.

My dear Miss Gregory,

It is my most sincere wish that you had as pleasant an evening as I did. Why, it seems barely possible that we parted just hours ago. I admit I find myself already missing your company and looking forward to our next conversation. It may be indelicate to state my feelings, but I warned you that I am not one to beat about the bushes. I would rather be rebuffed for my honesty than strung along because I am playing a part.

I have never found the rooms at Almack's as intriguing as I did yesterday evening. Your company brought wit and charm to the otherwise-stifling atmosphere. You were a vision of sunshine and enchantment in your gown. Being by your side reminded me of being gloriously out-of-doors beneath a warm July sun. I was charmed by your beauty and countenance.

Thank you for spending your evening with

me. I hope I did not wear out your slippers, or your feet, with my endless walking. If I did, I will replace them, of course. (I mean your slippers are replaceable, not your feet.)

I plan to call at Willowbrook Manor in a few days' time if it is convenient. I wish to visit with your father, and would also like to call on you as well. I will send my man beforehand to ascertain that this is an agreeable arrangement.

I will pull no punches, Miss Gregory. I do hope you are as eager to see me as I am to see you.

Please give my best to your parents. I am told your brother is also in residence. Please extend my good wishes to him, as well. It has been years since Oliver and I have seen one another. It would be most enjoyable to see how he is and hear what he is doing.

With fondest regards,
Nicholas Grayson

Lucie had received other letters from potential suitors, but none had been as eloquent and heartfelt as this one. There had never been one who had stirred her emotions as thoroughly as Lord Grayson's, either.

She only hoped the man would not be disappointed when he saw her again. It was a monumental task to keep up the appearance of being as bright as a ray of sunshine.

Too, she prayed Father would be well enough to receive the duke, if only for a short visit, and that the meeting would be an affable one. Being in the company of someone as filled with admiration as the duke was could only benefit her father.

The matter of Oliver being in residence, and receiving the duke, was something she would not allow herself to ponder. It was obvious that while the servants' information service worked remarkably well most of the time, there were still secrets that could be kept. She was thankful for that and glad her brother's infirmity had been closely guarded. If Lord Grayson had been aware of the condition, he would have no doubt been forthright enough to indicate as much. No mention bode well, and for that Lucie's relief was substantial.

Oliver had been whisked off and concealed somewhere on the estate. Not even Lucie knew where he stayed, although she suspected he was being kept, with his valet of course, at one of the guest cottages. Her initial impression had been that he was settled in the cottage by the brook, but Father had let it slip that was not the case so she was none the wiser about exactly where Oliver had gone. The temptation to seek him out preyed heavily on her mind and was part of her plan for the coming days, but thus far Aunt Lucinda, the Season, and Father's illness had kept her so completely occupied there was no spare time to spend looking for her brother.

Some excuse would have to be made to Lord Grayson in Oliver's regard. There was no way they could allow him to witness her brother's descent into…into what? It irked her that she still was not certain what ailed Oliver, but there was no use wasting energy she did not have over something she could not change.

Eventually she would find a way to help her

brother…

****

True to his word, Lord Grayson arrived at Willowbrook Manor three days after their evening at Almack's.

He was preceded by one of his uniformed servants delivering by fashionable carriage an embossed gray-and-silver calling card. Arrangements had been made and an hour agreed upon.

The morning of the meeting, another shiny carriage carrying two of the duke's servants, again in full, starched uniforms, arrived. This time they did not bear a calling card. Rather, each man carried an enormous arrangement of hothouse lilies. The scent from the bouquets filled the downstairs rooms with a sweet fragrance that brought the outdoors in and put the blooms in the gardens to shame. One arrangement had been addressed to Lady Gregory, the other to Miss Gregory. Both were duly admired.

The generosity of Lord Grayson seemed not limited to flowers. When the lilies had been set on a hall table, one of the men went back to the carriage and returned with a wooden box. The servant said the container was meant for Lord Gregory, and that the duke hoped the contents of the box might bring relief.

The carton held an assortment of teas. Leaves from across the globe, each variety tied in a petite pouch. When Lucie's father lifted the lid on the box, the aroma emanating from within was just as enticing as the scent from the lilies.

Lucie closed her eyes and imagined she was traveling, moving about the exotic locations where such high quality tea grew. In her mind's eye she experienced the thrill of seeing new and exciting things, and witnessing what she could only imagine.

By the time Nicholas Grayson arrived at Willowbrook Manor, Lucie was nearly beside herself with excitement.

She had chosen her dress with care, mindful of the duke's penchant for bright colors and partiality toward nature. Her sea green silk afternoon dress flowed like water in fountain, falling in soft waves around her ankles. The neckline showed her shoulders, but was not in any manner indelicate. She felt fully turned out, and ready to receive the only man who had captured her fancy.

Of course, Lord Grayson's visit was intended more for Father than for Lucie, but she knew she would have at least a short time with him. Why not make the best of every moment allowed her? She could hardly be faulted for thinking to make a good impression on the duke.

Aunt Lucinda had gone to stay at the dowager house at Waltham Hall for a day or so. It would have been nice to have her in one of the guest rooms, and able to offer an encouraging word where the duke was concerned. On the drive home from Almack's her sponsor had made no pretense about being monumentally overjoyed by the way her niece had garnered the undivided attention of the most desirable bachelor in the assembly rooms. It pleased Lucie to be able to make her aunt so animated and joyful. It pleased her even more to know that, for a time anyhow, she had claimed all of Lord Grayson's attention.

The smart-looking little chaise that pulled up in front of the manor was somewhat of a surprise. Lucie expected a man like the duke to drive—or be driven in—something more ostentatious than the light, open carriage. The top had been folded down, and the duke sat squarely in the center of the leather seat. He held the reins with ease, and directed the lovely Bay horse with a minimum of effort.

When he alighted, the duke brushed a hand over his curls and looked up at the front of the manor. Lucie gasped, and stepped quickly back from the second-floor hallway window.

How embarrassing, for him to see she watched his arrival. Goodness, but she hoped he did not imagine she had been waiting for him.

Before we have so much as exchanged greetings, I have put my foot in it. How unlike her that her enthusiasm for the gentleman pulled her to do things she would not have typically thought of doing. What influence did he possess? And why, without so much as a nod, did he bring a smile to her lips?

It was perplexing, but she was too happy at the duke's arrival to spare the riddle a moment's bother.

****

She was delighted to be invited downstairs eventually.

Lucie curtsied and, mindful of the way her hemline pooled attractively when she did so, held the pose an instant longer than necessary. When she rose and looked into the duke's eyes, she saw the effort had not been wasted.

Lord Grayson appeared pleased to see her. "Miss Gregory, it is an unparalleled delight to see you again."

Her parents looked on, so she gave a tiny nod. "I am happy to see you, as well."

Lord and Lady Gregory and the duke had been

locked in the library for three hours. It was unusual for Lucie not to be invited inside, especially when tea had been served, but she assumed there was a reason for her exclusion.

Once she believed she heard the front door open and close, followed by the sound of hoof beats, but when she cast a surreptitious glance out the window she saw the duke's conveyance had not gone. His horse had been watered and fed, and stood off to the side beneath the canopy of a shade tree. The chaise was parked neatly beside the animal, and both looked like they had not moved an inch in hours.

Now that she was finally asked to join the gathering, a flutter of uneasiness filled the pit of her stomach. She covered her midsection, feeling suddenly like she had swallowed a moth.

Do not be a goose! You are just happy, that is all. Lucie admonished herself for her foolishness. Perhaps it was good that Aunt Lucinda was not present to witness her flying her colors at the man's first smile of the day.

If the duke recognized her nervousness he gave no indication. He smiled again, staying on his feet until she folded herself into a chintz-patterned armchair that matched exactly the one her mother occupied. Lucie arranged her hands in her lap and watched their visitor reclaim his seat with a show of calm comfort. He sat on the far side of the hearth, in a brown leather chair that was, again, a match for another in the room. Lucie's father sat, his feet raised onto a worn leather footstool, in the mate.

As she glanced around the room, it caught her attention that both of her parents grinned from ear to ear. They glanced at each other, then at Lucie, and finally to the duke. There was a secret afoot, and Lucie knew without a word being spoken that she was the only one present who was not privy to the mystery.

The moth she imagined had taken up residence in her belly seemed to grow considerably—and quickly. She put one hand on her middle, keeping it in place as she contemplated the expressions on her parents' faces.

What could they be up to? And why were they keeping it from her?

Lord Grayson slapped a hand on his thigh, shocking Lucie from her reverie. He leaned forward, smiling, and said, "Miss Gregory, would you allow me to take you for a ride in my chaise? I brought it specifically to ferry you about, thinking you might enjoy such a diversion. It is not quite as sporty as Lord Bailey's fancy curricle, but it does move swiftly enough to be amusing."

The meaning of his words sank in. He had been at the lawn party at Waltham Hall and had obviously spied her riding with the Duke of Chichester. Was there a hint of sarcasm, or a touch of jealousy in Lord Grayson's voice?

"I say, Lucie my dear, I think you should take Nicholas up on the invitation. He is an expert horseman, and I am sure he can make even the clumsiest carriage fly like the breeze!"

Lord Gregory flashed an encouraging smile in her direction. It sealed the deal, as she could no more refuse the man a request than he could resist her tears.

"I would like that very much, Your Grace." Lucie felt very much like a mouse caught in a trap.

The three smug, satisfied grins that greeted her response were just a bit too content for her comfort.

They were up to something…but what?

****

The afternoon sun hung low in the sky, but there was still enough warmth and light to make riding in the chaise a lark. Father had been right about the duke's competence. They fairly sailed along the lanes winding through her family's estate.

Lucie kept an eye out for any sign of Oliver, but to her dismay, there was none. They passed near the cottage beside the brook, and although she knew it was wishful thinking, she stared into the sky for a tiny curl of smoke coming from the fireplace. Of course, she did not see one, so she chased the consideration from her mind and concentrated on enjoying Lord Grayson's company.

They rode for a half-hour in silence. Then, he directed the horse on a path leading toward the greenhouse behind the main gardens. It was a pretty spot, every corner of the lawn surrounding the greenhouse filled with cascading wisteria, tufts of larkspur and masses of peonies. The air was redolent with the scent of blooms, and the setting so private it was a simple affair to forget the manor house was only thirty yards away.

The duke reined the horse in beneath the canopy of an old, spreading oak tree. When Lucie was a little girl she imagined fairies lived in the tree. Now she admired it not for its fairies but for the cool shade it provided.

They alighted, and then walked to a wide concrete bench at the base of the tree. Lucie sat, glad to be out of the sun, but the duke remained standing for a long, silent moment.

"Your Grace?"

He appeared preoccupied, but their association was not close enough for her to ask what he had on his mind. Instead Lucie waved a hand over the empty space beside her. The bench had ample room to accommodate two or three adults comfortably, and she only occupied a small portion of the space.

The grin he flashed as he sat pulled one corner of his upper lip high and gave him a somewhat rakish expression. Lucie had in no way been interested in men who were not strictly on the right side of the tracks, morally or conscionably, so her experience with rakes, rogues, and scoundrels was severely limited, but she had heard stories, and those tales seemed to include tempting good looks and heart-stilling smiles.

"I would not think of refusing such a welcoming invitation." He gazed around at the flowers and glass-walled structure. "This is a warm, informal area. I think that if I had a spot like this on my estate, I might never be coaxed to leave it. In fact, I dare say I might want to climb up into this oak tree and take up permanent residence."

Lucie laughed, the spontaneous reaction to his having taken the words straight from her own head.

"Oh, it is funny that you say that. I spent many hours in those branches above us when I was a child." She pointed to the criss-crossing canopy over their heads. "I used to sit up there, and wonder why I couldn't just stay in the tree instead of having to go into the manor house, sleep in my bed when I'd be just as content to recline against the tree's trunk. I never did consider the thought that my room, with its walls and ceiling, provided more relief from the elements than this old tree could."

"I am not sure I would have considered rain or snow, either. The tree looks like it would weather any storm, and shelter anyone who trusted it enough to allow themselves to be cradled in it." Lord Grayson took a deep breath, and then added, "It might take a leap of faith to go from the comfort of your manor home to the untried branches of the tree, but there are times when leaping without considering overmuch the consequences of one's actions is a good thing. Don't you agree?"

They had stopped discussing the oak tree at some phase in the conversation, although Lucie was uncertain when the switch had actually taken place. It seemed polite to concede the point, so she nodded.

"Yes, a leap of faith…"

He gazed into her eyes, holding her captive with his dark, probing stare. His gaze wavered for a split second before he seemed to come to some kind of conclusion on whatever occupied his mind.

"Miss Gregory, I have a plan in mind that may sound somewhat startling, given the brevity of our association and the suddenness with which it is tendered. It is, however, a suggestion put forward with the most honorable of intentions and…well, the greatest hope that it will succeed."

Nervousness danced a highland jig in Lucie's belly. Part of her wanted to pull the plan from his lips, so she could hear it all the sooner. Another part, perhaps the bigger part of her, wanted to turn tail and run hard and fast for the safety of the manor.

Lucie was not prone to running from anything—or anyone. She kept her face calm, an inviting smile firmly fixed on her lips, and waited for Lord Grayson to come to his point.

It seemed lately that she waited more often than she liked for someone or something to do whatever it was they were about, in order that she be allowed to continue whatever she was up to doing. It was, she supposed, a woman's lot to wait for others to proceed, while she waited patiently for her chance to go forth. She was not sure she liked the idea, but less sure she cared enough to try to change the situation. Besides, there were already several "situations" on her plate. Adding another was nothing short of foolish.

Lord Grayson startled her when he took her right hand in both of his. The gesture was completely unexpected, but Lucie did not pull away. His hands were warm, and he held hers so tenderly a shiver of pleasure tore through her.

"Miss Gregory, I have spoken with your parents about the matter I am about to broach." He sounded confident, and intent on delivering his message, so she held her breath and waited for him to continue. "They are, I assure you, in total agreement that this is a mutually advantageous arrangement. They have also given their consent to the issue."

He raised one eyebrow, as if asking her whether she agreed, but Lucie had no idea what the topic of the conversation might be so she merely nodded and kept silent.

"Good," he went on, as if she had settled some matter between them. "This is, I realize, not the most desirous setting for an event of this magnitude, but as we can both agree, these are not ordinary times. As such, drastic measures must be taken, and conventions cast aside."

Drastic measures? Casting aside convention?
Good God, whatever can he be going on about?

Lord Grayson inhaled deeply, as if fortifying himself. Then, he looked her in the eye and, without further preamble, asked, "Miss Gregory, will you consent to be my wife?"

All power of speech fled her mind, and for several long, surreal moments, Lucie stared at the man sitting beside her. Either he had taken leave of his senses or she had lost her mind, because it sounded like he had just proposed marriage!

Just as I feared, Lucie thought with a sinking heart. I am imagining things. Insanity must run in the family!

Evidently she did not respond quickly enough for the duke's taste, because he dropped to one knee before her.

"I apologize. I completely forgot about this part. Leave it to me to make a mess at this juncture of our arrangement." He squeezed her hand, a gesture that reminded her that, for the moment at least, they were attached. "Miss Gregory, what I am asking is... Will you marry me?"

So she had not lost her mind!

"You—you are..." Lucie's voice trailed off as she attempted to make sense of his proposition. She found her voice and her wits at the same instant. "You are proposing marriage? Between us...you and me, married?"

He nodded, a relieved smile pulling his lips upward so handsomely Lucie's heart skipped a beat at the sight of him.

"That is *precisely* what I am suggesting, Miss Gregory." His smile disappeared, and he became somber as he rose off his knee and settled beside her on the bench again. "I know this is sudden—for both of us—but when your father suggested the alliance I saw the soundness of the idea immediately."

"Father? This is my father's idea?" Embarrassment brought heat to her cheeks.

Lord Grayson rushed to explain. "It was, I admit, your father's inspiration that put the plan in motion, but I quickly saw the feasibility of his idea. It is, certainly, advantageous to both families, and I believe it will be an arrangement that you and I can learn to live with. In fact, I believe we will become quite content with our circumstances. At least, that is my hope."

"You are telling me that you have schemed with my father to marry me, and I am simply expected to smile and thank you for your generosity? You must be out of your mind!"

Lucie pulled her hand from his and stood up, her spine as stiff as the whale bones used in her corsets. She would have stalked away, but Lord Grayson's words froze her in place.

"That is where you are wrong, Miss Gregory. It is, I am sorry to say, your brother Oliver who has gone mad."

She swallowed hard and willed the pulse galloping wildly in her neck to slow. When she felt in control of her emotions, Lucie turned to face him. The duke stood leaning against the oak tree's massive trunk. He seemed content to wait for her to speak.

"You know about Oliver?" The question came out as a strangled whisper.

"Yes. I have seen him. This very afternoon, with your father. It is a sad state of affairs, and I am very sorry to learn of the situation."

"How-how is he?"

The duke inhaled mightily, his shoulders rising nearly to the bottoms of his ears before he exhaled and dropped them back into place. He shook his head, sadness etched into his handsome features.

"As I said a moment ago, this is a sorry state of affairs." He paused, considering his words carefully. When he caught her gaze, she saw that Oliver's condition was even worse than she had imagined. "Your brother is quite ill. It is…that is, it seems to be some sort of affliction of the mind. He has…"

Impatience slammed through her with a force that nearly threw her off her feet. Lucie took two steps, and closed the space between them. She looked directly into the man's eyes and willed him to speak. Their short association had shown him to be honest—to a fault, perhaps—so she knew that he was someone who would give her the unvarnished truth about her older sibling.

"He has what? Tell me—please, tell me the truth. How is Oliver, really?"

"I will not lie to you, not about your brother or anything else." He raised an eyebrow, and asked, "Are you quite certain, however, that you are equipped to withstand the truth? It is, I warn you, not a fairy tale, and not for those with sensitive minds. Can you take hearing about the reality of your"—Lord Grayson shook his head quickly, then amended—"I apologize. What I meant to ask was whether or not you can stand the reality of our situation?"

Our situation.

Strength came when it was most needed. Lucie had believed that every day of her life, and the belief had served her well so why would she sway from the tenet now?

"I can take it," she said softly. Some of the force had left her, swept away when the duke had shouldered some of the heaviness she carried. "Please, tell me how my brother is doing."

"He is not well, I am afraid. There is some kind of mental imbalance. When we first arrived, your father and I, Oliver seemed calm. He sat beside a window, staring out at the view. His valet stated that he spends most of his day that way. The nights, however, are a different story entirely."

"The nights?"

Lord Grayson nodded. A lock of hair fell over one eye, so thick and curly it obscured his eyebrow. Lucie nearly swept it back, off his forehead and into place with his other curls, but his words stopped her.

"His nights are fraught with madness. There is no controlling him, no stopping the rampages, almost no protecting him from harming himself. In short, it seems that Oliver has, for some unexplained reason, taken leave of his senses."

Sorrow pierced Lucie's heart, and a soft groan escaped her lips. She stumbled, and would have fallen had the duke not put his hands on her shoulders and steadied her.

So Oliver has lost his mind! Oh, good Lord, why has this dreadfulness fallen on Willowbrook Manor?

"Are you all right? Do you feel light-headed?"

Lord Grayson's hands were solid yet tender on her bare skin. He held her close, but not so close they were in breach of propriety. His words, spoken with such concern and kindness, touched Lucie's heart.

"I am fine," she said, speaking into his chin. It was hard to meet his eyes now that she knew he had witnessed the insanity hidden beneath the attractive façade that was her heritage. "I assure you, I am just fine."

Lucie would have stepped back, but his hands held her in place. She looked up and met his gaze. Her expectations, had she any, about what she might see in the gentleman's stare did not include what she actually saw in his eyes. Compassion and sorrow, acceptance and understanding all telegraphed themselves instantly from his heart to hers. She felt less alone than she ought to, and more comforted than she felt she had a right to be.

How could he look so compassionately on her when he knew the truth? It seemed impossible, but the evidence of his humanity stared her straight in the face.

"It is my experience that those who insist they are fine are the ones who are furthest from that state." He hesitated, and then went on in a gentle tone. "Your father is ill, Miss Gregory. Your brother suffers a disorder of the mind and is quite unable to run Willowbrook Manor or properly care for you and your mother in the event…"

Lucie put a hand up and cut his words short. "I understand what you hint at, Your Grace."

"I hold your father in high regard. I will eventually have to wed, and while I know it is more romantic for marriages to be formed on the basis of—well, on the supposition of romantic endeavors, I find it just as agreeable to build a marriage on a mutual understanding. I did not come here today with a mind to propose to you, but when your father asked if I might not consider helping your family with my presence in it, I could not refuse him. He is, I am afraid, a hard man to turn down." Lord Grayson smiled. It was a small smile, but it cheered Lucie immeasurably. They did, at least, have one thing in common.

"You most certainly do not have to tell me about Father's powers of persuasion. I have never been able to say no to the man, not once in my whole life."

A pensive stare. The duke rubbed an encouraging hand along Lucie's arm.

"I hope that someday you will be able to say the same about me. It is a wise solution that will make your father happy and lay many issues to rest at Willowbrook Manor. I need a wife, and your family needs someone willing to keep its secrets and act in the best interests of everyone involved. I pledge that I will do so, if you will only give me the chance."

She believed him. It was written in his face that he had nothing but the best intentions at heart.

"Miss Gregory, I shall ask one more time… Will you do me the honor of becoming my wife?"

Family obligation ranked higher on Lucie's list of moral standards than did personal happiness. Consenting to marry the duke might not be a decision designed to satisfy her own wishes, but it would serve a greater purpose. Willowbrook Manor, Oliver, and her parents were much more important than any of her own desires or dreams for her future.

It was the right thing to do, so Lucie did not hesitate one second longer. She nodded, and forced a small, albeit wavering, smile to her lips.

"I will, Your Grace. I will become your wife—and I want you to know right from the start that I am grateful for your help."

So, it was settled. In the span of an afternoon, her future was decided.

In the end, it wasn't the Season, a wardrobe filled with stunning gowns, cotillions or affairs of her heart that determined the remainder of her life. It was, and always would be, madness and mayhem that instigated the most important match of her existence.

In the end, the heart hadn't mattered one whit.

It was the ramblings of insanity and the fluttering of an aged body that made her consent to marry the duke.

Chapter 7

"Are you certain, Lucinda Jane, that you do not want to hold the wedding at St. George's Church? It would be no trouble, my dear…no trouble at all."

Breakfast with her aunt was a rare occurrence, one Lucie only recalled having done a handful of times in her life. It was a familiarity that the elder woman did not deem in every respect proper, being from a generation where a day greeted in solitude was a day well begun.

When Ida Mae arrived at her bedside, poking her awake, with a note from Aunt Lucinda which requested her presence in the dowager countess's suite of rooms, Lucie knew something far removed from normal was afoot. She knew, as well, just what the prevailing topic for the breaking of their fasts was sure to be.

She was not wrong.

Aunt Lucinda frowned into her first morning cup of hot chocolate. She had just taken a sip and swiped her tongue delicately across her upper lip before she scowled. Staring into the cup like a gypsy gazing into a crystal ball, she seemed utterly occupied with the swirling brown liquid. Lucie would not have been shocked if, written in tiny words with cream, a prediction appeared.

Honestly, nothing shocked Lucie anymore. Not that she had ever been easily startled. While other women jumped at unexpected noises or unexplainable occurrences, she was typically calmer, her emotions steadier than most.

While she had, in her early teenage years, yearned for a proclivity toward swooning, it was a feat she on no account perfected. Lucie had only swooned twice in her life. Once, she had been stricken with a high fever in childhood. Her legs had buckled and she had, as she had been told by her mother and nanny, fallen to the kitchen tile like a sack of cabbages dropped off a table. Graceless, and jarring enough that her bruised knees required more attention than the spike in her body temperature.

The second experience had been just as mundane. She had been in her sixteenth summer and tripped over the hem of her walking dress. The tumble did not preclude her swoon; when she stumbled she grazed her palm on the edge of a sharp stone ledge, part of the retaining wall she had nearly fallen onto. The blood flowed fast and freely, its red stickiness rather reminding Lucie of the raspberry jam she slathered on her morning toast. The image, and the blood, had caused her faint. It had been as graceless as the first episode. This time, her walking companion, an acquaintance on summer holiday, told any and all who would listen that Lucie dropped like a stone thrown into a well.

Neither swoon made her feel particularly feminine. After the last episode, she resolved to do her best not to allow the action to repeat itself. Thus far, Lucie had been successful, although she could not help but feel that someday, under the right circumstances, and with the perfect companion, a swoon might be one of the closest feelings to being in heaven a woman could experience.

Aunt Lucinda's maid, Millicent, hurried to the table. It was placed before a window overlooking the front gardens and entrance drive, the same way the area in Lucie's room was arranged. The drapes had been pushed open, and sunlight streamed into the space.

There was no camouflaging the look of distaste on the older woman's face. Her expression seemed highlighted by the sun itself.

"Is something wrong, ma'am?"

"This chocolate…" Aunt Lucinda took another sip, and then pulled her features together in a look of supreme distaste. "Was it made to my specifications? And did you personally oversee its being whisked?"

A tiny spot of brown on the maid's white cuff hinted that she whisked the pot herself. She bobbed, and nodded. "Yes, ma'am. I watched every bit of your breakfast tray being assembled. The chocolate—"

The maid cast a tense glance toward the window, and Lucie wondered if she wished she was a groundskeeper instead of a lady's maid. For one wild moment, Lucie entertained the idea that Millicent contemplated jumping through the window and onto the stone drive below.

"Yes? Out with it, Millicent," Aunt Lucinda prodded. She placed her cup on the table with a small thud.

"I-I whisked the chocolate myself."

"Aha! That explains it!" The old woman looked as satisfied as a hawk with a mouse in its talons. Fortunately this hawk did not hold any interest in consuming its prey. "I knew you had a hand in this,

Millicent." The look she gave her servant softened as Aunt Lucinda picked her cup up and took another sip. "Yes, I should have known from the start this was of your doing. You are skimping on the sugar again, aren't you?"

The maid sighed. Then, with a nod, she said, "I am sorry, ma'am, but you know—"

"Yes, yes, I know. The doctor and his silly orders. You are just trying to take good care of me, I know that."

Aunt Lucinda and Millicent had been together for ages. No one knew which was older; it was a secret that might never be revealed. The lady and her maid were like a couple married for decades. Each knew the other's likes and dislikes, and each knew how to gain a desired response from her counterpart.

It had never been any save "Millicent" between Aunt Lucinda and the maid. No one had heard "Millie" or "Mill" or any other variation of the name. Her aunt's formal address toward her closest servant was as starched as the maid's uniform.

"Would you like me to add more sugar? It would be no trouble." Millicent reached to remove the chocolate pot from the table. A frown creased her brow, and she could not resist adding, "Although you know the doctor would not approve. Too many sweets in your diet, that is what he says. Not enough vegetables. Too many fruitcakes and puddings. But, if you wish for sweeter chocolate…"

"No, no, this is fine." Aunt Lucinda placed her empty cup on the table. "I'll suffer through the morning. You may fill my cup again, Millicent. It is not as if I am over-indulging now, is it? But do see whether my niece would like an additional lump—or two—of what I so dearly love but which is denied me."

The maid filled the china cup and managed to ignore the long-suffering commentary as only the highest lady's maid could. She kept her features bland. Holding the sugar tongs in one hand and the chocolate pot in the other, Millicent looked at Lucie and asked, "Would you like additional sweetener in your chocolate, miss?"

"No, thank you. It is fine the way you have prepared it, Millicent."

"Very good, miss." She filled Lucie's cup, placed the pot down in the center of the table, and then turned to her employer. "Is there anything else, ma'am?"

"That will be all. Thank you."

With a fast bob, the maid backed out of the room. She closed the door behind her, leaving Lucie and her aunt to enjoy their morning in relative silence.

Lucie was in no rush to return to the previous topic of conversation, so she helped herself to a scone. The basket was filled with blueberry scones, not the orange ones she so adored. Nonetheless, blueberry would have to do. When faced with the choice between tactfully dodging her aunt's idea of wedding must-dos and can't-live-withouts or blueberries, which incidentally had always reminded her of small blue beetles, Lucie chose the beetle-inspired scones any day.

She slathered more butter than she usually ate in a day onto a warm scone, and then took a bite. The sweet, buttery dough melted in her mouth, and the fruit was so warm and mushy it was less offensive than when eaten fresh from the bushes near the kitchen gardens. While she did not believe she would ever feel partial to blueberries, Lucie discovered they were at least tolerable.

Perhaps other things, more important issues like marriage to a man she did not love and a lifetime commitment undertaken for practicality rather than romanticism would become less distressing and more palatable as time wore on. Like blueberries, perhaps her situation would grow on her, even ever-so-slightly.

Lucie saw her aunt waited to broach the topic until after they were through eating, so she did what anyone in her situation would do. She took a second scone from the basket, sliced it open, and taking extra care to hide the berries from sight with a thick layer of butter, began to eat.

An exasperated huff shot from between her aunt's lips, but then they, as well as Aunt Lucinda, fell silent. The only sound in the room that Lucie could discern was her determined chewing and the steady throb of the headache threatening to erupt behind her eyes.

When she could not put one more bite into her mouth, Lucie wiped her hands on the napkin in her lap and said, "I do not want to argue with you, Aunt Lucinda. I know you wish me to marry at St. George's Church, with all the elite Mayfair crowd looking on and Hanover Square filled to overflowing with gawkers hoping to catch a glimpse of a long, lace train, but that is not"—she stopped and caught her breath, and then went on—"It is not what I wish for my wedding day. And, as this occasion has little of my own stamp on it, I do wish to retain some measure of control over what goes on. Most specifically, where the wedding is to take place."

The outburst she expected did not come. Instead,

Aunt Lucinda studied her over the rim of her cup for several long, quiet moments. Then, placing the cup on the table in front of her, the dowager countess nodded.

"I fully support your decision, my dear. I admit, I am your aunt—your *favorite* aunt, hopefully—" She waited, a coy smile playing around the edges of her lips, until Lucie nodded her head. "As your very favorite relation, I would, understandably, hope your special day be filled with only the best of everything. Flowers and food. Spectacle and grandeur. Of course, a gown made for a queen. All of it, Lucinda Jane—I want all of it, and much, much more, for you. Is that a crime? Shall we call the executioner at Newgate Prison, have him carry me off in leg irons?"

Lucie giggled at the mental picture Aunt Lucinda's words created.

"Of course not, Aunt. And just so you harbor no doubts, I would never, ever, not in a million lifetimes, allow anyone to carry you off against your will." Lucie reached out and grabbed the other woman's delicate hand in hers, and gave a fast squeeze. She held on tightly, and continued, "Believe me, that executioner would stand no chance against me. I may be small but I am determined."

"I know that, my dear. Believe me, it is one of the things I have known about you since the day you were born. You are very determined, Lucinda Jane." Aunt Lucinda hesitated, seeming to choose, then discard, her words.

Lucie watched quietly, knowing full well her aunt would not give up the conversation until she had said whatever pressed so diligently on her mind. Not even blueberries could save her from the advice of her "very favorite" aunt.

"You would rescue me, my dear. And I, with every ounce of strength in this old body, would rescue you, as well...that is, if you desire rescuing." Aunt Lucinda gripped Lucie's hand in a clench that underscored the meaning of her words. Then, as if she needed to clarify, she added, "Do you? Desire to be rescued, my dear? Because you know I will find a way out of your situation if you feel it is intolerable. I am proud of you—we all are—for putting family first, but there are times when family obligation crushes a person's spirit. That, my dear, I cannot allow. If, after consideration, you are regretting your decision, I will rescue you, Lucie. Just say the word..."

It was the first time her aunt had ever used her nickname, and it brought tears to Lucie's eyes. After the tension of the past days, feeling nearly choked by the relentless thoughts swirling through her mind and heart, joyful tears were a welcome relief. She sighed, and patted Aunt Lucinda's hand where it lay twined in hers.

"Thank you, Aunt Lucinda. I...I appreciate the offer more than I can say." Lucie chose her words more carefully than she had chosen anything else that morning. "But I do not need rescuing. No, I have decided what is most advantageous for..." She cleared her throat. "I have decided the most appropriate course of action, and I plan to adhere to it. I am quite certain it will all work out for the best. It will, I am sure of it."

"You are sure? Because it sounds like you are attempting to convince yourself of your certainty, my dear."

Lucie took a deep breath. "I am sure. Really, I am.

And I do thank you from the bottom of my heart for the offer of a rescue. It will not be necessary, but it is appreciated all the same."

Her aunt leaned back against her chair and crossed her arms over her chest. "So, no wedding at St. George's, then?"

"No. I am sorry, but I would rather be married here at Willowbrook Manor."

"I understand. There is no need to be sorry." Aunt Lucinda tilted her head. "Will the banns be read? That requires three Sundays, you know."

"I know. And no, the banns will not need to be read in church. Lord Grayson has procured a special license from the archbishop of Canterbury. We may be married where we please, and when it suits us."

A smile crept across the lined face on the other side of the breakfast table. Lucie knew the special license, with its costliness, appealed to her aunt's sense of extravagance.

"You will at least allow me the privilege of having a wedding gown made for you, won't you? It would mean so much to me, my dear."

With a sigh of relief, glad to have won the wedding battle so easily, Lucie nodded. "I would love a new gown for my wedding day, Aunt Lucinda. Thank you for that."

****

The library seemed empty when Lucie entered. Sunlight streamed through windows that had been pushed open, their heavy covering draperies gone for the day. They hung like voluminous, billowing sails over lines strung amongst the trees in the back gardens, looking like a Navy armada of land-locked ships but in actuality only a fleet of household linens.

The room was in the early stages of being cleaned. All of the downstairs spaces, and some above stairs as well, would receive the same treatment. Weddings did not come often to Willowbrook Manor. The house was being readied for the noteworthy event.

Lucie did not wish to witness the sweeping, dusting, polishing, and upholstery-beating that would shortly take place in the room. All she wanted was a book to take outside with her, so that she might find a secluded place to pass the morning. She did not know what she wanted to read, but it did not matter.

The library was a marvelous place. All she ever had to do was trail a fingertip along a row of gold-embossed spines, their contents holding boundless possibilities for exploration, for leaving her own life behind in exchange for another, more dramatic and far more interesting one, to find the magic in the room.

Time was short. Servants in the front parlor were just finishing their ministrations and would soon find their way to the library. Lucie did not hesitate. She walked straight to the shelf where poetry found its home and stood before it.

"In the mood for a good read? Perhaps looking for this?"

As she turned, Lord Grayson placed a slip of paper between the pages of a book. She recognized the book instantly. He held *The Odyssey* in his hands. The slender volume looked like a child's book of verse in his large, capable grip.

"Lord Grayson. I did not know you were here." Lucie curtsied as her mind scrambled for something suitable to say. "I-I supposed I was alone. The, uh…ah, yes, the servants will be here any minute now. They are cleaning the rooms for the, uh…"

"For the wedding," he finished.

"Yes."

He looked, as ever, impeccable. Today he wore riding clothes, his inexpressibles so snug about his hips that she noticed for the first time how well-muscled and trim he kept himself. The shoulders beneath the gray riding jacket were wide, his waist slim and his hips and legs powerfully built.

It was no wonder Lord Grayson excelled in sports. His was a physique made for such strenuous activity. It was funny how dancing and strolling did not show his form to its complete benefit, when something as commonplace as conversing surrounded by books did.

"So, were you searching for Homer?" He held the book out to her, but she did not accept it.

Instead, she turned and removed a book from the shelf behind her—at random. She clasped it to her chest with a smile and a tiny shake of her head.

"No. Thank you anyway, but I did not pop in to fetch Homer. I only wanted this, and now that I have found it I will take my leave."

She was not running, exactly, or at least that is what her mind said as her feet began to move. But whichever held control over her body, be it her feet or her head, was of no consequence.

Lucie had only gotten two steps closer to the doorway when his hand shot out and caught her. The grip on the bare skin of her upper arm was warm and firm, but it was not demanding. She could have disengaged herself if she had chosen to do so.

However, Lucie did not try to gain her freedom.

She stood as still as one of the plaster statues scattered about the corners of the room. A small sigh escaped her as she looked into his eyes.

"Why do you run from me? I mean you no harm."

The words were simple but they sounded pulled from his heart. Lucie did not know what to say, so she kept her gaze locked on his and waited. When it became obvious that she would not respond, Lord Grayson continued.

"I did not come here this morning in search of a book." He smiled, and then placed *The Odyssey* on a table beside them.

"No? You did not wish to borrow a book? What, then? A cup of sugar, perhaps?" Teasing him was fun, especially when he threw his head back and laughed.

It was the first carefree moment they had spent together since his proposal. The room around them seemed brighter than it had earlier, and Lucie's heart felt lighter than it had in days. Perhaps their arrangement might work out with no trouble at all.

She noticed he had not released her arm, but it was not a disagreeable connection so she did not bring attention to the fact. Lord Grayson's touch sent tremors of delight dancing along her skin. Lucie supposed it was static in the air that encouraged the oddity. The servants must have riled the dust around them to such a state that it affected those nearby with shivers and such.

What a smile. I could watch him smile every day of my life.

"I confess, I did not come to Willowbrook to borrow anything, although if I had the time I would like nothing more than to enjoy a bit of sugar with you—in my tea, that is." He grinned, almost laughing again when she caught his joke and smiled. "But my reason for this impromptu call is a purely selfish one. I realize you are busy during these days before the ceremony, but I hoped you might spare me a few minutes."

He looked down toward Lucie's chest. She colored, realizing his gaze might be on the neckline of her dress, but before she could protest his insolence, the duke read the title of the book she held off its spine.

"*Sonnets for Seafarers*—why, I never would have guessed you might choose that volume as one of the last of your maidenly pleasures. I fear my own library does not contain a copy of that book, so I have never read it. Perhaps after we are wed I will borrow it, and see what poetry exists for sailors—or is it written by sailors?"

The inquiry smacked of interest and politeness, but Lucie's mind was a complete blank. She had never read the book, either, and would have loved nothing more than to ignore the question.

Social protocol demanded she answer, so she said airily, "Oh, it is something that one must read for oneself. Poetry is never…that is, I believe poetry is meant to be experienced rather than relayed."

He eyed her for a moment, and then did something that caught her off guard. The hand on her upper arm relaxed, but Lord Grayson did not let go his hold entirely. Tracing a fingertip across her skin, he considered her words.

"Are you saying you believe poetry cannot be shared?"

"Oh, no, not at all," she said, covering her verbal misstep with a vigorous shake of her head. It was almost impossible to think with his finger drawing circles on her skin. Goose bumps rose along her arms but she ignored them. "I believe poetry—much of it, that is—is meant to be shared."

"As do I," he said smoothly. Lord Grayson's apparent calmness made Lucie feel far jumpier by comparison.

"Yes, well…as I was saying, there are poems that are more pleasing when shared, but there are others that are best read alone and with…uh, with oneself."

Get a grip! He is only a man, for goodness' sake! How can I let him affect me thusly? It is…why, it is supremely ridiculous.

Which was precisely how Lucie was beginning to feel. Ridiculous did not appeal to her so she stiffened her spine and hugged the book closer against her bodice.

"If you will excuse me, I have things that require my attention."

The sound of voices grew louder. It would only be a matter of minutes before the servants, their mop buckets and polishing rags in hand, descended upon them. Lucie did not want to set tongues wagging. Letting the staff see her alone with the duke could only bring conjecture, and she definitely did not want to add to the speculation surrounding their brief, almost non-existent, courtship and hasty marriage.

Lord Grayson must have heard the voices, as well, because he dropped his hand from her arm and reached inside his jacket. He pulled out a black velvet box and handed it to her. Lucie did not think; she accepted the slender box with a surprised gasp.

"This is what I came to see you about." He looked askance at her, nodding to the box she had made no move to open. "I realize we do not know each other well enough yet to have confidential knowledge of each other's favorites but I do hope you like what I have chosen. It is, I believe, customary for a gentleman to give a gift to his betrothed before their wedding day. A promise, of sorts..."

Lucie inhaled sharply. She had not expected this. Not only was the duke's presence, and his gift, bolts from the blue, but the sincerity evident in the dark eyes he trained on her gave both items importance that tugged her heartstrings.

"Are you going to open it?" He gestured to the closed box. "I think we have only a short time before your staff makes our private moment public."

With shaking fingers, Lucie pulled the hinged top away from its base. When she saw what lay on a bed of black velvet, all thoughts of the staff flew from her mind.

The choker was exquisite. Three strands of brilliant red coral beads, held together with a gold filigree clasp, calmed her shaking fingers and stilled her galloping heart. The piece was enchanting, the fiery hue of the beads bringing to mind images of faraway, exotic locations where spicy and hot were the norm.

"I am told that red is the rarest shade of coral, and that these pieces were harvested in the Aegean Sea, off the coast of Greece. The waters there are so warm the coral reefs grow enormous, some reaching unheard-of proportions. It is a beautiful place, Greece, a land full of ancient secrets and modern treasures."

Lucie loved the way the duke's eyes lit up when he spoke about what he had seen. For one instant, she was there with him, experiencing the mysteries and beauty at his side.

"I have never been. It sounds beautiful."

Lord Grayson did not hesitate. "It is. We will take a trip one day in the not-so-distant future, you and me alone, and explore the land to your heart's content. I love to travel, and I hoped you might feel the same."

It was nearly beyond imagining!

"I have never gone anywhere," Lucie admitted. The jewelry box was still open in her hands between them. *Seafaring Sonnets* had been tucked under her arm when she opened the box. Now, it fell to the floor with a loud smacking sound that slapped the romance right out of the moment. "Oh! How could I be so clumsy?" She glanced down at the small volume but made no move to claim it. Bringing her gaze back to the duke's, she offered a tiny smile and said, "I suppose the lure of travel and adventure swept me away."

"So you are agreeable to travel, then?"

She nodded. "Very agreeable."

If he only knew how agreeable!

"Good. It is settled, then. Once we are married, and have sorted family matters out, we shall embark on a journey. We will..." His voice trailed off, the last breath a near rumble.

Lord Grayson's dark eyes held her gaze so closely Lucie wondered if it was possible to tumble headfirst into the velvety depth of him. His penetrating stare brought heat rising from her bodice and up her neck. The room felt too hot for the first week of July, but she knew the warmth that overcame her did not emanate from the world around them, but rather from the world growing between them.

The duke cleared his throat. "As I was saying, we will have an adventure, darling. We will see the world, and perhaps we shall find ourselves in the process."

It registered that he had called her "darling" but before a response fashioned itself in her head, he brought attention back to the bridal gift.

"Many cultures attribute certain properties to coral. It is said to ensure good health to the wearer and provide vitality as well as material gain. It has been used, coincidentally, for its protective powers by seafarers." He bent and retrieved the book from the floor near her feet. Placing it on the tabletop beside *The Odyssey*, he smirked. "Your choice of reading material seems pre-ordained, doesn't it?" An answer was unnecessary, so the duke went on. He looked down at the choker before he caught and held Lucie's gaze.

"Coral is also said to increase the commitment between a husband and his wife. It is my fervent wish that we enjoy a strong, mutually satisfying marital bond." He paused, but Lucie was too stunned to reply.

"I do not know what color gown you will wear for our special day, but I hope this gift will match. It would bring me great pleasure if I were to see the choker around your lovely neck. It is beautiful, but it will pale against your vibrancy."

Panic seized her when his curly mop inclined slightly and he leaned closer. It seemed he might steal a kiss, but just when she was about to close her eyes to receive his touch, the sound of buckets being deposited in the hallway outside the library door made her eyes open and her brows lift high.

Lord Grayson heard the noise as well. His own eyes widened, not in surprise but in abject annoyance. A grimace pulled his lips stiff, but he straightened.

A small, tight smile, then a polite bow.

"Thank you for receiving me, Miss Gregory, on such short notice."

"Ah…thank you, Lord Grayson, for…for everything."

Chapter 8

Miranda and Amy had slept in one of the guest rooms at the manor house the night before the momentous day so they were there early to keep her company. She was grateful for their presence. Their sisterly advice, pearls of wisdom regarding everything from undergarments to cosmetics and the laughter that flew swiftly among them drew her ruminations toward a more general attention for the day rather than the finer details that had brought her to this auspicious occasion.

From her earliest memories, Lucie had assumed that on the day of her wedding she ought to be filled to overflowing with love and respect for the man of her dreams. She had believed her betrothed would be the one man set upon the earth made specifically for her, and she for he. Her dreams were that they complete and complement each other perfectly. He would, in a word, be her destiny.

She had always held very definite ideas about the man himself, as well. He would be handsome, smart, with a flawless sense of decorum and polite to a fault. His tastes would vary considerably, and he would be thoroughly competent both indoors as well as out. An accomplished sportsman, the man of her dreams would ride like the wind, sail like the breeze and be strong enough to carry her safely through any storm.

The point uppermost in her musings, from her

earliest recollection, was her prince would not only capture her heart, he would treasure it above all else. It was childish, she knew, but she had always believed that when she married it would be for love, and no other reason. After all, why else would someone proclaim before God and their nearest and dearest to cleave to one person for the rest of their days? Any excuse save soul-gripping, heart-stopping, all-or-nothing love would be sheer insanity.

There was that word again. Since learning of the true nature of Oliver's affliction, Lucie had worried she, too, would go mad.

Surely what she planned to do this very morning had some semblance of madness about it. The scheme was a clever one, but could it take the place of true love?

I hope he does not expect more than I am able—or willing—to give. She half-listened to the two sisters discuss hairstyles as she gazed out the window. For the moment she was free to let her mind wander. It gravitated like a magnet on iron shavings to the ceremony that would take place in two hours' time. How could it not?

I will not give my body to a man who has not claimed my heart. It is not something I can do—not willingly.

While Lucie did not know her betrothed all that well, she knew him well enough to guess he would not force her to do something she did not want to do. He would not take what she did not wish to give. She felt certain of the point and safe enough that she had no compunction about going through with the ceremony.

As if reading her mind, Amy leaned forward and

asked, "Tell me, Lucie…is Nicholas the man of your dreams? Is he the one you have been waiting for your whole life through?"

She stared blankly at her companion. *Nicholas?*

Then, she caught the meat of the question.

"Oh—Nicholas! Why…why, of course he is the man of my dreams. How could he not be? You have known me long enough to know that I would not consent to marry unless it was to…well…to a man who met my criteria." There. That was close enough to the truth that she did not feel she had told a Canterbury tale.

Amy's long auburn ringlets fell in tight curls across her shoulder. When she spoke, they bounced against her white dressing gown, like bold splashes of color against the pristine background.

"You were not surprised, then, when he made an offer?"

Surprised? That does not begin to cover it, Lucie thought with a wry grin.

She did not want to weave a fabric of faradiddles but she could not tell the absolute truth, either. The middle ground seemed safest for the moment, so she went for that position and hoped it would serve her well.

"I dare say any woman is surprised, to some extent at least, when a man proposes marriage. After all, it is not a union to be entered into lightly, as we all know."

Lucie suppressed a shiver. God knew, she was not tripping down the aisle with a kerchief over her eyes. The restless nights she had spent recently pondering the plan were a testament to her out-and-out lack of flippancy regarding the joining together of the Gregory family with the Graysons. There was very little lightness to anything about the day. The only real satisfaction was knowing the union would take a burden of worry off her father's shoulders. Hopefully, it would in some way—although she did not see how—also make Oliver's life better.

Not having her older brother present at her wedding ceremony was another thing she had never dreamed would happen. It seemed that along with the promise of security some of her preconceived notions, and a few dreams, had been cast by the wayside.

The piper must claim his due.

"See, Amy? No one casually jumps onto the matrimonial cart." Miranda cast a worried glance at her sister. When Amy rolled her eyes, she grew more vehement, shaking one index finger at her sibling. "I saw that! You think you are in love with Lyle, and perhaps you are, but you should still exercise caution where matters of the heart are concerned. The way you keep going off with him…honestly, sister—do you want to be the talk of the Town?"

A defiant shake of auburn curls was the initial reply. "I cannot believe you set such store in what people think, Miranda. Let them think what they will; I do not care a groat. What do I care if they have the correct impression or not? Those who matter know who I am—and what I will or will not do—so let the others spin tales." Amy pensively twirled one curl around the tip of her finger. Then, she grinned. "They had just better not let my Lyle hear a bad turn of phrase. He will draw claret should anyone be cork-brained enough to insinuate that I am anything but a woman of quality."

Lucie did not wish to take sides, but she could not hold her tongue, either. There was too much at stake, and she cared such a great deal about both sisters, that to sit silently was impossible.

"I am not certain that the threat of a bloody nose is enough to protect your reputation, Amy." She searched for a tactful turn of phrase, but could not find one so Lucie simply told the truth. "You will be ruined, my friend, if someone spreads a faradiddle that you are doing anything not entirely seemly. Doesn't it matter to you that once you are ruined, it will be nearly impossible for you to regain your good standing?"

The question struck a nerve.

A long, drawn-out sigh escaped the spirited sister. She gazed first at Miranda, then at Lucie. Finally she stared at the floor between her feet. Worrying her lower lip between her teeth, she did not say a word for some time.

When Amy looked up, there were tears in her eyes. "But we are on the high ropes! Really, we are so passionately enamored with each other that there is almost nothing else on my mind but Lyle!"

"Oh no, Amy. Not on the high ropes. You have not—heaven forbid...you and he...?" Miranda placed a hand over her heart.

To their enormous relief, Amy swatted the notion away with one hand as if it was an annoying insect.

"No, of course not. I know you think we are doing more than playing cards when we slip away together, but you are wrong, dear sister." Amy flashed a superior smile. "Faro. That is it, I assure you. Lyle is teaching me the strategy involved in the card game."

Faro involved wagering on the order of cards as they were dealt from the bottom of the deck. Lucie had never played the game, but she did not believe strategy had anything at all to do with the outcome of the diversion.

"I did not think there were any tactics involved in Faro," Miranda said quickly. Lucie smiled inwardly. Leave it to Miranda to find a hole in Amy's explanation. "I thought it was all the luck of the draw."

Amy sighed, plainly put out by the line of questioning. "It is a game of chance, you are right about that. But…there is some logic, and some counting of the cards as they are drawn. You see, every card pulled is one less card that may be pulled it the future. And if you know the cards pulled and are able to recall them… Oh! Why are we wasting breath on a card game? If you really are interested, I will teach you someday."

"You are the one who brought Faro up," Miranda pointed out.

"Yes, I did, but I did it just to show you that Lyle and I have not done one thing that I would not do in full view of all of London. Of course, I have allowed him to steal a kiss or two, but that is all. We are on the high ropes for each other, but our feelings are all strictly without offense."

"That is good to hear." Relief showed clearly on Miranda's face. "Then what is the point of bothering Lucie with all kinds of questions about romance? After all, it is her wedding day. She would probably much prefer to talk about her romance than hear about yours."

They turned to Lucie, but when Amy opened her mouth, most likely to apologize for monopolizing the conversation, Lucie cut her off before she uttered a word.

"I do not mind in the least. I am happy to hear about your romance, Amy. Lyle sounds a true companion, and if my guess is correct, you have already lost your heart to him. Is that so?"

Heaving a dramatic sigh, Amy flung herself back in her chair. Waving her hands in the air, she exclaimed, "It is definitely the case. I cannot escape him, even when we are not together. All the time, it is Lyle. Lyle at daybreak, first thing as I am opening my eyes. Lyle, his face so dear to me that I cannot keep it out of my mind, in the morning while I take a walk. Lyle while I am sewing, while I am reading, while I practice the pianoforte. *Lyle, Lyle, Lyle!* It is like he never leaves my heart, as if I am overcome—and willfully so, I assure you—by the man. Oh, I am too enamored by far! I do not know how I will stand the days until he and I can be married. I hate to say this, but I mean no offense and it is the truth, Lucie…"

Amy paused, looking too embarrassed to go on but she had raised Lucie's curiosity.

"Do tell, please. What is the truth you try so hard to conceal? I promise, I will not take offense."

"I must admit that I would give anything to trade places with you this morning. How I wish it were my wedding day and I were the one being married instead of you. I know it is selfish, but I cannot help how I feel. I am so in love with Lyle that I feel I might burst if we do not get to our engagement and the reading of the banns and finally…" Amy curled one long tendril of hair around her fingertip as she spoke. The habit had been with her from childhood. "I know I should not be envious. It is not a comely trait, but I cannot tell a falsehood, not to you and Miranda of all people. I do so envy your getting married, Lucie. Really and truly, I do."

Lucie swallowed around a sudden lump in her throat. She had not had any fits of the vapors or severe moments of doubt about what she was going to do this day but Amy's heartfelt admission stunned her. It gripped her heart, making it nearly painful to breathe.

And I envy you, my friend. Oh, how I envy the love you and Lyle share. Would that I could find the same I would be happy every day of my life...

****

The wedding ceremony was history almost before Lucie realized it had begun. What the entire household had been turned upside down preparing food, rooms and costumes for was over in a matter of minutes.

Lord and Lady Gregory both looked relieved when Lucie stood beside the duke before Rector Crane. Amy and Miranda, in matching cornflower blue silk gowns, were bridesmaids. Aunt Lucinda, smiling as benevolently as if she had personally arranged the advantageous match for her favorite niece, sniffled delicately into a Brussels lace handkerchief.

Lord Grayson's family was in America on extended holiday. so they missed the event. He did not seem to mind at all that he was the only Grayson in the room.

Clad in an expensively-cut charcoal gray morning suit, the duke was handsomer than any man had the right to be. Lucie's breath hitched when she walked into the drawing room and saw him standing before the clergyman. His gaze swept up her body, from her slippers to her face. She colored at the attention he afforded her while the duke made no attempt to hide his pleasure at seeing her in her wedding finery.

Aunt Lucinda and her seamstress had outdone

themselves. The yellow gown was as soft as spun silk, with a sheer golden underskirt and form-skimming, heavily embroidered panels that parted with each step Lucie took to reveal a tissue slip of a still lighter hue. The effect was elegant yet dazzling. Lucie had never felt as beautiful as she did in the gown. She suspected she might never feel the same again—not even if she lived to an advanced age.

The wedding necklace brought a burst of color and a hint of warmth to the ensemble.

Strangely, there were no butterflies fluttering about her tummy when she stepped into the room. She had expected to feel like fleeing, but instead her feet, in their gold satin slippers, moved her quickly to Lord Grayson's side without requiring any conscious effort on her part.

Before the Rector had a chance to begin the ceremony, Lord Grayson leaned so close his whisper stirred tendrils of hair beneath her white lace veil. A shiver shot up Lucie's spine as she inhaled the scent of his cologne.

"You look like liquid gold, darling. I am enchanted, thoroughly enchanted…"

From that moment on, Lucie could think of nothing else. The duke's words echoed in her mind as her heart galloped in her chest.

It was, quite simply, the best morning of her life.

Chapter 9

Willowbrook Manor was large enough that the newlyweds had their choice of accommodations. There were two guest cottages which would have housed them adequately, and the manor itself boasted a suite of rooms in a secluded wing which seemed ideal for a newly-married couple.

Under normal circumstances, Lucie would have gone to live at her husband's home, but their state of affairs was anything but ordinary. The duke had kindly consented to live with the Gregorys for a time, with the hope of getting matters sorted out at Willowbrook Manor.

While Lucie would have liked to remain in her childhood bedroom, she knew that was not feasible. It was ideal for one person but not spacious enough for two. Since Lucie had no intention of sharing such tight quarters with the duke, she chose the secluded suite of rooms.

Her things were relocated during the wedding ceremony. She had given orders to Ida Mae regarding the duke's trunks, as well.

Weariness made Lucie's steps leaden as she and the duke climbed the stairs to their rooms.

The manor was quiet. The small party of wedding guests had long since departed, each bearing an extra slice of orange cake with butter cream frosting. Lord and Lady Gregory were in their private rooms, and Aunt Lucinda had removed herself to the dowager house at Waltham Hall, saying her work for the Season was complete.

Lucie pushed open the doorway to the sitting room. A fire crackled in the grate, and candles sent puddles of soft light into the space. The room was large but welcoming, and she began to enter ahead of the duke.

A hand on her arm stopped her. She turned, confused by his touch.

"Is something wrong, Your Grace?" Lucie used the formal term of address with her new husband simply because she had not yet figured out what to call him. She had been mulling over the prospects all afternoon, but none seemed to fit so she had solved the problem by not calling him anything. Now that they were alone, the politeness slipped out.

It brought a fleeting scowl to the duke's face but he concealed his displeasure behind a small, conciliatory smile.

"Not wrong, precisely. But I fear you have forgotten one of the wedding traditions, darling."

Darling. He had used the endearment all day. It warmed her as completely as a fire burning within her, but she would not allow the word, or the feeling it inspired, to influence her. It was, she assumed, merely the duke's way of playacting, of putting the servants' curiosity to rest and announcing to all within hearing distance that he claimed her for his own.

Lucie knew better than to be deceived by a word. He could call her anything, but that did not make it so. There were enough words in the English language for the duke to choose from; "Darling" suited their purposes adequately enough, and would help conceal the charade they had entered into.

She just wished he would not use the term when they were alone. It was unnecessary to keep up the façade, and it did have that warming effect on her which was, at times, wholly disconcerting.

"Marriage tradition?"

A self-satisfied grin alerted her of his intentions a scant half-second before he reached for her. Lucie put her hands out in front of her and placed them on his chest. She tried to push him back, but the action was futile. He was built as solidly as a stone wall, and was just as immobile.

"Oh, no…I do not think…"

The duke brooked no protest. He lifted her into his arms and held her close against her chest. He did not bother to hide his amusement.

"Oh, yes. I do think," he said with a wide grin. "I do think we should follow all traditions and wedding protocol, don't you? This is the only wedding day we will ever have, and this moment is my only chance to carry you over the threshold, and take you from your old life into your new."

Lucie was tired, but she was not so fatigued that her senses did not respond to the nearness of the man. He was her husband but this was the closest they had ever been. His strength was not surprising, because she had guessed that a man who wore his clothes so well and moved with such sure-footedness and grace must have a superior physical stature.

It was, however, the care and gentleness with which he cradled her body that caught her off guard. The few times she had imagined this moment it had been with a nameless, faceless bridegroom. She had pictured the gesture more a lift-and-toss motion, the way the gardener moved heavy sacks of produce from the gardens to his wheelbarrow. No amount of pondering could have let her know how safe and secure she would feel in her new husband's arms. She definitely did not feel anything at all like a sack of potatoes!

When he hesitated, and seemed in no hurry to step into their rooms, Lucie shyly met the duke's gaze. He had been watching her, waiting, it seemed, for her to look up at him.

"Well?" When he spoke, Lucie felt the rumble of his voice in his chest. It was a strange sensation, feeling as well as hearing him speak, but she did not have time to dwell on it. "Are you ready?"

"Ready?" She sounded like Cedric, and hated the fact. Mustering all the dignity she could summon under the circumstances, Lucie cleared her throat and asked, "Ready for what, may I ask?"

If he was put off by her attitude, he did not show it.

"Are you ready to leave your old life, and begin your new one?"

It was kind of him to ask, but Lucie did not believe it was necessary. Moreover, while she did not mind being held by the man, it also seemed unnecessary.

Besides, did she have a choice? Ready or not, the die was cast.

"We've already made our vows, so don't you think it is too late to ask that question?"

The look on his face was serious, but it was not one of annoyance so she steadily held his gaze as he studied hers. Then, a shrug that lifted her, and pulled her more closely against his chest.

"It is never too late for anything. Never."

Sincerity, in his words, facial expression and action shocked her. She stared silently at her new husband for a long moment. There were layers of meaning in his statement. Lucie recognized the detail but was too worn out to mull it over. Perhaps another time, after she got to know the duke better, his meaning would show itself. Now, though, hardly seemed the right time to examine the force behind his words.

She had more pressing matters to deal with. The duke looked as if he could stand in the doorway all night long and well into the coming week, if necessary. He had not shifted her weight in his arms once and did not seem strained by the effort of holding her. Granted, she was a slender woman, but still, they had been as statues for several minutes now.

She could not resist a bit of teasing, despite her weariness. "How long will you stand here like this?"

"As long as it takes."

"As long as it takes for what?"

She instinctively brought her arms to cover her chest when he lifted her, not allowing herself to wrap them around his shoulders. The gesture had seemed too familiar, but now as the duke chuckled and shook her body slightly, she put an arm around his shoulder. It was, she assured herself, just for good measure. Falling onto the floor from such a height would certainly produce a painful bruise, so why take that chance?

"I will stand here until you tell me you are ready, unreservedly committed, to moving from your old life and into your new one. When you are prepared, and indicate as much, then we will go forward together." He flashed a quick grin. "Until then, we will stand right here."

She spoke before she could censor herself. "Does it really make a difference what I think or how I feel? Does it, really?"

The grin disappeared but the reply came softly, gently. "It matters. It matters a very great deal."

It is true, she realized with startling clarity. *He means what he says. It matters to him that I am committed to this marriage, despite its nature.*

"Then, I am ready." Lucie gave a small nod.

"I hoped you might be."

The duke stepped over the threshold with Lucie in his arms. He stood just inside the doorway for a moment, looking down at her with a satisfied smile. Without turning, he kicked the door shut with one foot, and then strode across the room toward the fireplace.

When she thought he would put her down before the fire, he held her tightly. Too unsure of herself to pose a question, Lucie concentrated on not moving or making a fuss, on just allowing the moment to present itself and hoping beyond hope that whatever happened, she would not make a cake of herself.

"Are you warm enough?" The duke asked solicitously.

"I am. It is…ah, it is quite warm in the room."

The fire and candles added heat that might have been welcome had it been September, but the early July night provided sufficient warmth on its own. The glowing details had been added for ambience, and, Lucie supposed, to make the space seem inviting. Romantic.

"Are you too hot?" The duke's gaze swept over her

face. She felt his hands tighten slightly on her, and he pulled her more closely against him. "You do not have a fever, do you?"

"No, of course not! And I am not—I mean, I did not say I was hot, did I? I just made the observation that it is warm in the room. And it is, isn't it?"

"Hmmph." It was an ambiguous reply, but one he had given before in other instances so she assumed it was one she would have to eventually learn to decipher. Without another word, he turned on his heel and went through to the next room, still carrying Lucie in his arms.

Candles, as well as a fire, burned in this room as well, but they were smaller and there were less of them. A soft glow illuminated the space and its furnishings.

The most prominent piece of furniture was the bed. It stood in the center of the room, between two tall, wide windows. The four-poster, ornately carved piece was generations old. Lucie's parents had spent their wedding night in the bed, as had her grandparents and great-grandparents. The coverlet had been turned down. A heavily embroidered nightdress, lace at its collar and cuffs, lay across the foot of the bed.

The duke walked slowly toward the bed. When they were a foot from it, he set Lucie down on her feet. For a second her knees felt wobbly, so she held onto his shoulders for balance. When she regained her equilibrium, she released him and took a step back.

Now that there was distance between them, she missed the closeness of him. Pride kept her from closing the gap between them.

He swept one fingertip gently over the ruffled edge of the nightdress. Then he turned his gaze on her.

"Beautiful. You are beautiful." He came close enough that he did not have to stretch when he reached for her. Lucie held her breath as her husband ran a slow fingertip across the beaded choker snugged against the base of her neck. "I am glad you wore this today. It pleases me immensely."

"I-I am grateful for the gift. It is lovely." His touch was light but it brought such divine sensations. "Thank you."

She could not look at him for fear he would see the effect he had on her shining in her eyes. Lucie struggled against feelings and emotions too numerous and unfamiliar to make sense of.

The duke placed a hand beneath her chin and lifted her face. She felt he might kiss her, but he gazed into her eyes and said, "There isn't anything in this manor as lovely as you are, darling."

That endearment again, and after such a flattering statement, unbalanced her. Lucie did not know what to say. She opened her mouth to speak, but no words came to mind so she closed it again. A second time she opened her mouth, and again she found her mind completely blank. Snapping her lips together and pulling the lower one between her teeth, she stared into his eyes feeling like a complete ninny.

The duke chuckled. He placed a tender finger across her lips, sealing them. The gesture, so intimate and unexpected, chased away the statement slowly forming in her head.

"I fear I may have frightened you with my forthright manner." Candlelight reflected in his dark eyes. He looked lit from within with a fiery glow. "I warned you, I do not tell lies, have no patience with falsehoods, and believe in being honest at all times. You said you agreed with me, did you not?"

His finger still lay across her lips, so she nodded.

"Good. Our marriage may be a bit unconventional, but it is still a marriage. From the first moment of our wedded life together, the new life we just leapt into when we crossed the threshold, I want one thing to be perfectly clear between us."

The duke hesitated, as if weighing his words. Their gazes were locked, so Lucie saw the indecision in his eyes and felt the gravity of his feelings. He took his finger off her lips and let his arm drop to his side. It was both a relief and a loss. Lucie wiped her tongue over the spot he had touched.

The waiting was killing her. Squaring her shoulders, and preparing herself for whatever marital demand he might make, she asked, "What is it? What do you demand from me?"

"It is not so much a demand as a request. All I ask, all I truly want, is for you to be honest with me."

"I have never been anything but! How dare you insinuate otherwise?"

He hurried to soothe her ruffled feathers. "I am not saying that I suspect you of doing so. Quite the opposite, in fact. Our discussions have been almost brutally honest, to tell the truth. There is…well, there is much that we have had to discuss that I wish had never been an issue."

She knew without being told that the duke referred to Oliver, and his madness, as well as her father's infirmity.

"Agreed. It would be wonderful if certain issues had never been brought between us. But, if wishes were horses…"

"Beggars would ride," Lord Grayson finished smoothly.

He smiled, and she returned the gesture. Lucie saw, for the first time, that he looked worn out from the festivities and excitement of the day. It was, she was almost embarrassed to admit even to herself, one of the first times she had taken a good, long look at the man.

They had been side by side during the ceremony. Then, through the wedding breakfast she had sat at the long dining table, again at his side. Afterward, the afternoon was spent out-of-doors, with everyone involved in the day free to enjoy the food tables, play lawn games, or simply stroll about the gardens.

Lucie had spent most of her afternoon talking with Amy and Miranda. Their presence provided an insulating layer between herself and her new spouse, one that Lucie needed since she did not know what to say to the man whom she had just married.

So, her day had been spent either by the duke's side or, she was loath to admit but it was the unvarnished truth, avoiding him. Neither had presented an opportunity for close examination. Now that the man's face was just inches from her own, she could see the day had taken its toll on him.

So I am not the only one at sixes and sevens, and worn out from the nuptials.

"Apparently you and I listened to the same childhood rhymes," Lucie said, her heart considerably warmer toward him than it had been a minute earlier.

"It would seem that way." The duke plowed his fingers through his hair, a careless gesture that emphasized his attempt to find common ground between them. He sighed, and then said, "Whatever either of us wishes was the case, we have some highly unusual, and unfortunately stressful, situations to deal with in the very near future. My expectations for the successful reconciliation of all issues depends—no, it *demands*—that you and I work together. We need to trust each other, and I cannot trust someone who may not tell the truth when asked. I realize this may be a strange nuptial night request—"

"I have none to compare it to, so I do not know precisely what sort of requests are standard on the nuptial night," Lucie said calmly. His show of nerves and apparent weariness made him seem less formidable by far. The case of collywobbles she had been experiencing the whole day through vanished like a wisp of smoke on a stiff breeze. "Whatever you request will be 'normal', at least for us. Moreover, there are so many other items between us that could be deemed 'strange' if anyone knew of them that what you ask is not nearly unusual enough to be termed thusly."

The duke's relief could not be hidden, although he did not attempt to do so. "We are in accord, then. We will deal fairly and honestly with each other at all times." His voice softened as he went on. "I have…I have, well… It is with very good reason that I hold honesty a virtue above most others. Some other time, perhaps, we shall discuss the subject further and I will, honestly—even though it does not put my family in a favorable light—tell you why this is of paramount importance to me."

"Certainly, Your Grace."

The instant the address sailed past her lips, Lucie wished she could swallow it back.

The face that had just relaxed frowned again, and the tone that had just softened growled, "Good God, I am your husband, not your landlord. You cannot continue to call me that, Lu—"

He stopped, furrowed his brow. His scowl was slight, but his aggravation patently clear.

"Do you prefer Lucinda Jane, as your aunt refers to you, or would you rather be called Lucie? I suspect I know which is preferable, but I would rather be certain. Which is it?"

"Lucie."

"As I thought." All trace of annoyance disappeared as the duke tested out her name several times. "Lucie. I rather like that. Lucie. Yes, a very friendly sort of name. Trustworthy and companionable. Lucie...yes, it flows."

"You make me sound like a cat with a bad case of intestinal distress."

He threw his head back and laughed. Lucie could not help herself; she did the same. The sound of their shared amusement filled the room so thoroughly it was as if a cool, sweet-scented puff of air had swept through the room.

Shaking his head in amazement, the duke grinned. "I believe you and I will get on famously, Lucie. Your wit and intelligence impress me. Very much."

The compliment pleased her. It was better, she had always believed, to not be held as someone with more hair than wit.

"Thank you, Your—ah, thank you." *I should bite my tongue—or keep my mouth closed! I am too tired by far to speak without getting myself into a bumblebroth.*

"Ah, you *are* quick," the duke said appreciatively.

He stared into her eyes and, in a subdued voice, said, "I rarely have to provide options to people regarding how to address me. It is usually apparent and socially ordained. You, however, are my wife."

A thrill shot through her at the word. Was it fear or excitement? Lucie had no way of knowing for certain, so she kept her features carefully arranged and listened.

"Therefore, you have several options open to you. My Christian name is Nicholas, which is a fine way of addressing me. If you are so inclined to be on more familiar terms, Nick also does the job. I have never been fond of Nicky, but if it delights you I am sure I can, in due time, grow accustomed to responding to the name."

He waggled his eyebrows mischievously, sending a second charge up Lucie's spine. Again, she had no idea why it happened, only that it did.

"Of course, darling Lucie, you may decide a more intimate nickname suits your purposes. There are many…dear…darling, which I am fond of and suits you well so that one is, I must point out, already taken… Let us see, the other informal terms of address are so numerous one can hardly be expected to list them all, especially on such short notice, but let us see… There is dear heart, which to me sounds bulky but again, I am adaptable…of course cupcake, pudding, and other food-inspired endearments come to mind. The only one I am particularly not fond of is sweeting. If you could choose another form of address, I would appreciate it. That word—it just does not sit well with me."

The grandfather clock in the hallway chimed midnight. No wonder they were tired. Their wedding day had come and gone, and they were still afoot.

Lucie stifled a yawn with the back of her hand. It had been coming on for a while but she had not wanted to appear rude, so she had swallowed it repeatedly. Now, there was no holding it back.

"Excuse me," she said with a tired smile. "I fear it has been a long day."

The duke reached out and cupped the back of her head in his hand. His fingers wove into her hair, working so slowly it took her a moment to figure out what he was doing. Then, as hair pins began to fall to the floor at her feet and soft curls and tendrils of hair fell in waves onto her shoulders, it hit her.

"You are so beautiful," he murmured appreciatively. "I am a very lucky man, to have wed a woman with wit and comeliness. Very fortunate indeed…"

His head lowered toward hers, and she recognized his intention. Although she had never been kissed, aside from the brief touch of lips during the wedding ceremony, Lucie was no fool. She knew how it was done, and had an idea of what a new husband would expect from his new wife following their first kiss.

With a small gasp, she avoided his kiss by taking a step back.

A look of shock crossed the duke's face, but he allowed it to be seen for barely a second before he straightened. "Are you all right?"

"I am fine," she admitted. A few hairpins remained in her curls, so she pulled them out and held them tightly in one fist. "I am just tired. It has been a long day."

The duke sighed, and then nodded his agreement. "You are right. It has been quite a day."

He looked at the bed and appeared ready to sit down on it so Lucie quickly pointed to the doorway at the far end of the room. Firelight's glow spilled onto the floor, lighting the way to the other space.

"Your room is over there. I had your things unpacked, so all should be in a state of readiness. If you require anything, just let me know and I will see that you get it." She colored, heat flaming her cheeks.

Thank God it is dim in here.

"I, ah, meant that if you require anything for your comfort—I mean, if you need extra linens or towels, or a pot of tea brought to your chamber…anything of that nature—let me know and I will see you are accommodated." She felt like a fool, chattering on and on. And he had just complimented her on her intelligence! What an irony!

Amusement twitched the corners of the duke's lips upward. "I decipher your meaning. I am certain the room—and its towels and linens—are just fine."

"If they do not suit your needs—"

"You shall be the first to know." He stepped away, and then bowed slightly. As he turned toward the open doorway, he said, "Remember, that by the morrow I will expect you to have come to a decision."

"A decision?" The question came out as a squeak.

In the doorway, the duke turned and nodded. "Yes, a decision. You need to decide what you will call me from this day forward. We are in this new life together, remember? I refuse to go through the rest of our days with my wife calling me 'Your Grace'. I am your husband. Please decide what you will call me."

A tiny nod was all Lucie could muster, but it seemed to satisfy the man.

"Good. Thank you." He started to walk into his own room, but only got a step inside before he stopped and turned back to look speculatively across the room at her. "Good night, Lucie."

"Good night," she said softly.

Chapter 10

"Good morning, Lady Grayson."

Dropping to a curtsey in the center of the upstairs hallway, the maid held a tidy pile of folded laundry against her starched uniform. She obviously waited for a reply and would have received one more expediently had Lucie realized she was the one being addressed.

"Ah…good morning, Mary Jean."

They parted, the maid headed toward the far end of the long corridor and Lucie for the front staircase. She made it there without meeting anyone else, for which she was glad. The one encounter startled her, as it had been entirely unexpected. She had spent most of the previous night staring at the ceiling in her new room, struggling to find a comfortable position in her new bed and mulling over what to call her new husband when she next saw him.

She had given no contemplation whatsoever to the new name she had acquired less than twenty-four hours earlier.

So many new things to remember, so many decisions to make… Good Lord, I hope I did not jump from the frying pan and into the fire.

The dining room was empty when she arrived. She had expected to see the family around the table. The idea had seemed rude when she contemplated having a tray sent to her, so she had dressed, preparing herself to assume the new role she seemed destined to play.

Only there was no one with which to practice being the new Lady Grayson, no one to remark how enjoyable the wedding festivities had been. There was not even a crumb on the sideboard, or a teapot beneath a cozy.

"Lady Grayson! Oh, I did not expect to see you standing there." Tillie, one of the kitchen maids, entered the room with a large vase of fresh flowers in her arms. She placed it on the sideboard, dropped to a curtsey, and then said, "Good morning, ma'am."

"Good morning, Tillie." Showing her disquiet before the servant would have been a mistake, so Lucie nonchalantly sniffed one of the blooms, taking her time to appreciate the scent of peony as it filled her head. When she straightened, she asked, "Where is the family?"

"Oh, they are all on the terrace overlooking the rose garden. Lady Gregory said it is too hot to eat anywhere else. That stretch of patio is so well shaded, you know. And the flowers fill the air so nicely with their perfume, don't they?"

"Yes, they do."

"Will that be all, ma'am?"

Lucie gave a quick nod, and the young woman bobbed before she left Lucie alone in the room.

So that was it...the breakfast party was on the terrace. With a mix of anticipation and sudden shyness at seeing her new husband again, Lucie hurried through the large rooms.

She lingered at the open French doors, and watched the scene before her. Her parents, smiling and looking better than they had since Oliver had returned home, sat on one side of a wide glass-topped table. The duke, a

142

tea cup held loosely in one hand, sat across from them. Beside him, an empty chair.

Lucie stepped outside. At the sight of her, the duke rose to his feet, put the tea cup down on the table, and came to her side. He brushed his lips across her temple in greeting, the touch as gentle as a fluttering butterfly wing.

"Good morning, darling." His words were as smooth as silk, the endearment rolling off his tongue as if he had been using it with her forever.

"Good morning...Nick." She caught the satisfaction in his smile and retuned the simple gesture. Trying to act as if she, too, spoke so casually with him without having to take a deep breath beforehand, she went on, "Nice weather we are having this morning, isn't it?"

The weather never failed to provide a middle-of-the-road topic of conversation. He smirked, apparently aware of her attempt to find a neutral item for discussion.

"It is indeed, a nice morning we have been blessed with." Nick put a hand beneath her elbow and escorted Lucie to the table. He pulled out the remaining chair and waited while she sat. Then, he seated himself beside her and, without hesitation, reached for the large china chocolate pot and poured her a cupful. He placed the cup in front of her with a broad smile. "Perhaps we might take a walk this afternoon. I would love the chance to see more of Willowbrook's grounds. I am told there are a number of secluded areas."

The hot chocolate scalded her throat as it went down. She had not intended on taking such a huge gulp, but his words startled her so completely there was no way to avoid doing so.

Lucie sputtered indelicately, grabbing a linen napkin off the table and using it to cover her mouth.

Her parents passed an amused look between them that she did not miss.

Wiping a tear from the corner of one eye, she gasped, "Secluded areas?"

If he knew what she was thinking, Nick gave no indication of such. He looked perfectly at ease, and unperturbed by her outburst.

"That is what I have been told, that there are several secluded glades beside the brook and clearings in the forested areas near the gardens. I wonder if we might investigate some of those out-of-the-way spots. Actually I hoped you might consent to be my tour guide and show them to me yourself."

Nick flashed a bright smile, sending a flock of butterflies fluttering through her midsection. He was so incredibly handsome, and so self-assured. Lucie was still having a difficult time grasping the concept that she and the duke were husband and wife.

Before she could comment, he went on. "I have taken the liberty of asking in the kitchen for a picnic basket. I know it is premature, since you have not agreed to go on the outing with me, but I thought that if you do consent to be my guide, the least I can do is feed you for your effort. It is, as I am sure you now realize, the perfect picnic spot that I am hoping to discover."

When she had gotten her coughing fit under control, and had dabbed away the ensuing tears, Lucie placed her hands in her lap. The big white napkin she still clutched in one, but the other was empty and rested over the one holding the napkin. She was not entirely sure she would not need to avail herself of its size and absorbency again before her breakfast was behind her. The way the duke made proclamations—without warning and so completely unexpected—meant that she might choke a second, or even a third, time. Better to hold tight onto the napkin.

Nick reached between their chairs and placed his hand over hers. With an earnestness that would have melted even the coldest, hardest heart, he asked, "Would you do me the honor of going exploring this afternoon, darling? The day is clear, the sky is bluer than blue, and the cook has promised all of your favorites."

"My-my favorites?" How on earth could he know her tastes? It was almost entirely too much to comprehend.

"Certainly, all of your favorites. I have requested watercress sandwiches, without crusts, of course. I have asked for a fruit salad, with lots of those bitter Mediterranean oranges you have such a fondness for. Of course there will be beef sandwiches, for me. And, along with some assorted cheeses, breads, and fruit, the cook has promised a surprise. It is, I believe, something she is baking special for our first picnic together." He stopped, tilted his head questioningly and asked, "Is there anything else you want? I am sure I can coax someone into packing it for you into the basket—that is, if there is any room left in the basket. Just tell me, darling, what you would like and I'll go this very minute and request it for you."

Nick began to stand, but Lucie waved him back down. She shook her head, overwhelmed by his kindness and apparent willingness to get to know her better and, perhaps more importantly, please her.

"No, please. What you have in mind sounds divine. I could not ask for more."

****

"This is my favorite place on the estate." Lucie swept a hand lovingly over the wide marble balustrade as they ascended the stairs which lead to a broad stone patio. "I remember running in circles around here when I was a little girl, just going as fast as my small feet would carry me, laughing at the top of my lungs and not stopping until I was near to being sick. Our nanny, Gretchen, never tried to stop me from running in circles. She said Oliver had done the same thing when he was my age, and it had never done him harm so she assumed my constitution was equally strong."

"I can see why you love the place."

They walked, not ran, around the perimeter of the small circular structure. There were no windows in the walls of the building, so there was no way to peek inside. It was built of pink marble which had been imported from Ireland. Every few feet, a thin vertical line ran from the bottom of the exterior wall to the top, where it joined the roofline.

"I believe every estate should have at least one Folly. Don't you?"

Lucie took a chance bringing Nick to the one place she considered her own, the particular spot where she had never felt any of the troublesome things children, and then teenagers, feel. The truth was that hers had been a fairly calm existence, and any worry had been minimal. But this was her special place, and she had never shared it with anyone. By the time she was old enough to follow the trail through the forest, her nanny had been banished from accompanying her to the Folly.

Bringing Nick here was a giant leap of faith. She was not sure he could ever completely understand how she weighed the decision to direct him to this part of the estate when they had set out on their afternoon tour.

Marriages required foundations. He demanded honesty. She wanted trust—to be able to trust someone with her feelings and ideas, and with the things that meant the most to her. And she wanted to be trusted.

I hope he sees more than a silly little building. I shall be able to learn so much by the way he responds to my magical spot. Dare I hope he understands?

"This is enchanting." The sound of Nick's palm rubbing against the smooth marble brought joy to Lucie's heart. She had run her own hands over the blocks too many times to count and had felt the same burst of wonder she saw on his face now. "I have never seen one of these buildings this close up before. It is a marvel of craftsmanship and almost too perfect to be made by human hands. Your father supervised the building of the Folly?"

"No, it was my grandfather's idea. I am told it was a gift to his little boy, my father. Father says that when he was small he would often hide in the Folly with a sack filled with blocks and another filled with cakes and biscuits. He would play until someone came looking for him to take him back to the manor. He said..." Lucie sighed, because her own feelings echoed her father's so completely she understood them as well as if she had been the first to experience them. "He said he felt the world ended over there, at the edge of the clearing, and that his own sanctuary, his very own private world, was here."

Nick kept still for a long moment, and she was grateful for the silence.

"He played out here? On the patio?"

Since his appreciation seemed genuine, she had no problem letting him further in on the building's secrets.

"No. He played inside the Folly, where no one could see him. That is what I used to do, as well, except my sack was filled with books, and the other held sandwiches and fruit rather than cakes and biscuits. Oh, all right…I admit, I did snitch the occasional handful of biscuits."

His laughter blended perfectly with the sound of birdsong.

Nick ran a hand along the nearest vertical line. He pressed his thumbnail into the groove, and then shrugged. "How? How does one get inside this little hideaway? And—I have to ask before I die of curiosity—is it as dark in there as I imagine it is? Or are the windows as well hidden as the entrance door appears to be?"

"Oh, you are smart! I will show you the way inside, but only if you promise never to divulge the secret to anyone else."

Their walk around the building had brought them back to the point just beyond the stairs leading up onto the patio. They stood in silence, staring at each other while he contemplated her request. She could feel Nick's breath on her cheek, warm and steady, and wondered if she had made a mistake. Perhaps he could not be trusted. Perhaps he would bring scads of people to the secluded getaway. Perhaps—

Botheration! How can I doubt him, after all he has done for my family? And how can anyone with such dark eyes be anything other than trustworthy?

It was preposterous, but she could not help herself. The duke's eyes hypnotized her, pulled her right under his spell, and held her captive. Lucie did not doubt she would give him anything he asked when he studied her thusly.

Solemnly he crossed his heart with his fingers, then held his hand in place over the mark he had just pantomimed making.

"I swear I will not violate your confidence. Not about this Folly...not about anything at all. Trust me, darling. Please."

How could she not? She took Nick's hand and led him around to the far side of the Folly. Then, she permitted him entrance to the one spot she guarded as exactingly as she did her heart. He followed her inside, and the door swung on soundless hinges, closing behind them.

Chapter 11

When Lucie entered the library, both her husband and her father were deep in conversation, seated in identical brown leather armchairs before a roaring fire. The air was warm but a fire in the grate was a custom her parents enjoyed, whatever the calendar season, so the logs burning gaily was a nightly occurrence.

She crossed the room on silent, slippered feet, taking a deep breath as she approached the men. The day had been splendid, and she had high hopes for the evening ahead. Nick had been a wonderful afternoon companion. She hoped he would be as interesting a dinner partner.

As she grew closer, Lucie heard snippets of the conversation. Nothing made sense, as she had no way of knowing what had already been discussed and what was yet to follow, but one thing was plain: Oliver was the topic of conversation. She heard the words "madness", "docile" and "morose" before her father spotted her. When he did, the conversation died as both men rose to their feet.

"My dear, you are a vision in that dress. And the glow about your eyes—why, marriage must agree with you." Her father pulled her into a fast hug, and Lucie noted when he stood back that he, too, looked like marriage—*her* marriage—agreed with him. There was brightness in his eyes, and color in his cheeks that had not been there just a few days ago. It warmed her heart to see the old gentleman looking more like himself and less like an invalid.

If this is what my marriage has brought, it has already been well worth the effort. I will do whatever it takes to keep Father looking this well.

Nick took one of her hands in his, then leaned down and touched a kiss to her temple. He gave her hand a squeeze, and smiled admiringly at her. His gaze swept down her body, and she felt the touch of his examination as fully as if his fingertips trailed after his gaze.

"Your father is right, darling. You look ravishing tonight. You wear that gown beautifully. It is amazing, is it not, that the fabric is nearly the exact shade as your Folly?"

Lucie moved to the settee, taking her hand from her husband's grip. She sat down, arranging the pale pink panels falling from her empire waist artfully around her. The dress had been chosen with infinite care. It was a favorite, because it did remind her of the special little building. It pleased her to see that Nick had made the connection.

She murmured her thanks while she attempted to conceal her satisfaction at the impression she had made. Pride could only lead to downfall. Best to simply accept their flattery without allowing it to give her a swelled head.

The men reclaimed their seats.

"Oh, so Lucie has shown you the Folly, has she?" Lord Gregory gave a knowing nod, one she recognized from having lived with the man her entire life. Her father was not surprised by what she had done.

Somehow, he had expected she would share the Folly with Nick.

"Just today. We had lunch inside it, actually. It is one of the most perfect buildings I have ever seen. I was very much impressed. Your father certainly had good sense when it came to construction. It was remarkable to see something so entirely unexpected in that precise spot. Yes, I am deeply awed by the treasure."

Nick's appreciation of the Folly made Lord Gregory puff up like a turkey in full feather. He took a tiny sip from the half-inch of port wine the doctor allowed him each day, and smiled so widely his thick, bushy white moustache stuck out past his ears on either side of his head.

"I love the place, myself. I haven't been out to it in years but I would like to see it again soon. It was always such a magical spot…"

With a glance toward Lucie, then putting his attention on the aged gentleman, Nick said, "If you would like someone to accompany you one day to the Folly, I would consider it a great adventure to do so with you. Perhaps you can tell me more about how it was built, if you recall any of the details. I decided once I got inside your Folly and saw the way the sunlight streams though the windows set into the high ceiling, that I shall have one built on my estate, as well. That way, when Lucie and I take up residence there, she will have a place of her own with special ties to Willowbrook Manor."

A lump the size of a guinea fowl caught in Lucie's throat. How could he be so generous? So kind? It was completely unnecessary—but so delightful!

Nick turned to face her and caught Lucie's astonished stare with his own calm gaze. "I know whatever I build for you will never have the history of your Folly here at Willowbrook, but I do hope you will find a way to make new memories, and build a new history, with a new Folly. I have already sent word that I wish my head groundskeeper to begin making inquiries about securing some pink Irish marble similar to what this Folly is built of. That is, unless you wish the new building to be a different color entirely—would you prefer that, Lucie? The building is for you, so you should have all the word about how it is built."

Her mouth opened, and then snapped shut. She felt like a fish thrown onto a dry pier with no hope of finding its way back to water. How could he so completely disarm her? And he had done it in less time than it had taken her to dress.

Lucie struggled for composure. Every word that entered her head seemed hardly adequate, yet she had to say something. Both her father and Nick were staring at her, and waiting for an answer.

"I am touched by the gesture, Nick. I-I confess, I do not know what to say…a Folly is a large undertaking. I would not wish you to assume such a big effort simply on my account."

I sound like my corset is tied too severely. Why do the words that matter most elude me?

Nick raised his brows when she gave the stiff reply. "There are many *large undertakings* in life, my dear. Some of them are very much worth the exertion. I assure you, any effort I expend on your account will be very well worth it in my eyes. So, when you have some time to think it over, perhaps you might decide on a color for your new Folly. I will relay a message and ask that inquiries be held up until you advise me of your decision."

A clamor at the doorway precluded Lucie's being obligated to respond. They turned their attention to the crowd entering the room, and temporarily left the Folly discussion behind.

Amy and Miranda, Lady Gregory, and Aunt Lucinda all arrived at precisely the same moment. Greetings were exchanged, hugs given and received and general inquiries made about the state of everyone's health and, of course, the disposition of the weather.

Before everyone could find a seat, a second clamor occurred in the doorway, this one not as chaotic as the first had been. Two of Lord Gregory's oldest friends, Lord Farwell, the Duke of Groton, and Lord Taylor, a lesser earl, arrived. Each man had one of his sons, both of marriageable age, with him, so the dinner party grew to eleven.

Lucie's mother caught her on the side of the room while pre-dinner refreshments were being served and said, "Dear God in heaven, save me. Lucie, whatever shall I do?"

Her mind was still on Nick's Folly, but her mother's distressed countenance sent images of marble and form from her mind. She placed a hand on her mother's arm, feeling for any sign of clamminess or illness. With both men in the Gregory family seriously ill, the thought of Lady Gregory falling under the weather was almost too much for Lucie's heart to bear.

"What ails you, Mother? Shall I call for Doctor Fairwater?" Lucie placed a steadying hand beneath her mother's arm, readying herself for a catch if the need arose.

"Doctor Fairwater? Whatever for?"

"Mother, what hurts?"

"What hurts whom?"

Shaking her head in exasperation, Lucie spoke slowly and patiently, as if to a young child. "Mother, you asked what you are going to do. I can only assume you are ill, and in need of assistance. Unfortunately I cannot help you unless I am aware of what ails you. So, what hurts?"

Lady Gregory drew herself up to her full height, pulling her arm from her daughter's grasp with a snort.

"I am not under the weather, my dear. Apparently your newly-acquired marital state has given you feelings of motherly intent." A small smile and a sigh punctuated the observation. Then, Lady Gregory brought her eyebrows together into a thin line. "While I appreciate your concern, my fit of nerves is not caused by infirmity. I am fine, Lucie—or, rather, I will be once I figure this mess out."

"Whatever is wrong? What mess are you talking about? Why, all seems to be in fine order."

Lucie gazed at the group assembled in the room.

Everyone seemed to be having a delightful time. There were jokes being told, confidences being exchanged and enough laughter to indicate no one— except her mother—was at all unhappy.

"Yes, of course. Everyone is having a good time *now*. But what about when dinner is served? What then?"

"Mother, what are you going on about?" Lucie was losing patience. She realized, as her gaze caught her husband's across the crowded, noisy room, that she wanted to be beside him instead of stuck in the corner trying to decipher the source of her mother's distress. "Just tell me the problem, so we may find a solution and get on with the evening."

"There are eleven dinner guests." A dramatic sigh underscored the fact. "It is, as you well know, less-than-advantageous to host a dinner party with an unequal number of guests. Of course, the division between men and women should ideally be divided so as to encourage spirited conversation but, at this late point, I could not give a fig if the twelfth at the table was canine rather than human! No, I do not mean that literally…it is just that I feel so inept having dinner with eleven rather than ten or twelve. Whatever shall I do?"

Lucie was saved by the arrival of number twelve to their dinner table. Rector Crane, the man who had performed a wedding ceremony on the premises barely a day earlier, arrived behind the butler, Hastings. Hastings's announcement of the unexpected—but entirely welcome—visitor sent Lady Gregory scurrying to pull him into their party.

To her unequalled relief, Lucie found herself alone, her ears still ringing from her mother's excited chatter. She relished the chance to find her bearings, and regain her composure.

His voice no longer took her entirely by surprise, so she did not jump when Nick sidled up beside her and whispered in her ear, "You look to be in a brown study, darling. Is everything all right?"

Lucie hurried to reassure him, touched by his concern more than she could say. "I am fine. I was just thinking, that is all."

He eyed her speculatively for a long moment, and

then asked, "Is there anything you would care to discuss? Anything I might assist you in solving?"

She nearly shook her head, but realized before she did so that it would cut the conversation off. That was not her intention, so she said, "No, there is nothing that particularly needs to be solved, but thank you for asking and offering your help. I was simply thinking about my mother, and about the dinner party—and, mostly, about how important it is to feel successful at what you do."

"I do not follow your line of thinking. Please, go on so I may understand."

Now that she had begun, explanations came without difficulty. They were, quite simply, a matter of telling the truth.

"My mother takes great pride in running Willowbrook Manor to the best of her ability. She has taught me how to run a home properly, as well."

Nick nodded, as if any other scenario was altogether ludicrous. A small glow of satisfaction at his confidence in her ability to assume a manor's responsibilities flickered within her. Emboldened by his demeanor, Lucie went on.

"When it became clear that there was an unequal number of diners for the upcoming meal, Mother became quite visibly distressed. At first, I saw it as silly, but now that I ponder her reaction, I see she was not upset by the actual number of people who might sit around the dining table. She was disturbed by the thought that, with a disproportionate number of persons at her table, there might not be sufficient stimulating conversation. She worried that her guests, and her family, might be deprived. It upset her so fully she was nearly in a state."

Lucie put a hand on Nick's forearm. The muscle beneath his dinner jacket was unyielding, and she held on longer than she needed to simply because the feel of him was agreeable. When she realized her hold on his arm pushed the limits of decorum, Lucie released him—reluctantly.

He gave her a grin that sent her heart skittering in her chest. His gaze showed he not only had tolerance for her household prattle but understood clearly the crux of the discussion.

"You are saying that my mother-in-law was upset because, in her eyes—if in no one else's—she had not done an adequate job of providing good company and conversation this evening, because circumstances dictated that the dining table be one member shy of the correct number of diners?"

"That's it, yes." She loved it that he understood, without demanding additional explanations. "My mother takes her position as lady of the manor so seriously that one small miscalculation or empty dinner chair sends her into a near-fit."

"Quite admirable, I think, to take one's situation to heart like that." Nick glanced around the room, and when her mother looked up, he caught her gaze. A wide smile and fast nod of approval brought a becoming hint of color to Lady Gregory's cheeks. "Quite admirable, indeed."

"Yes, of course. It is not as if my mother is high in the instep—quite the opposite, in fact."

"Your mother does not possess one haughty bone or allusion of false pride in her body," Nick agreed. "And I do not believe pride is such a poor virtue, if you must know. Taking pride in an accomplishment or in providing happiness to another is not something to be considered rag-mannered over. Satisfaction is not a bad thing, not when it is fairly earned. What do you think, darling? Is satisfaction a virtue or a sin?"

His words ensnared her, and she saw he had done so intentionally. A teasing grin softened the ambush, but it was, still, a mousetrap—and she was the mouse.

"Are you playing with me? Is that what this conversation has become, a word game?" Answering a question with a question often worked to ensnare the hunter, so Lucie tried the tactic. She added an engaging flutter of eyelashes, hoping to turn the tables on him.

Nick looked deeply, seriously, into her eyes. For several heartbeats, the room around them faded into obscurity. The only person she saw, the only voice she heard and the only opinion that mattered stood directly in front of her. Their bodies were so close they nearly touched, and she could see the rise and fall of his broad chest as he breathed. A wild notion to reach out and lay her hand over his heart shot though her mind but, thankfully, she regained her senses before she made a fool of herself.

His voice, and the words he spoke, made her own madly beating heart thud even more distinctly.

"I admit, Lucie darling, I am toying with you. You enchant me, and your quick wit amuses me. You do not mind, do you?" Nick took one step closer, and put a hand on her shoulder. "If you do not like my teasing, just say so and I will try to contain myself."

Lucie did not want Nick to change anything he did or said. She was having too much fun getting to know him, and the thought of one bit of their relationship being put to rest was the furthest thing from her mind.

"No, don't change, please." Her voice was a whisper, but he was close enough to hear her words. "I am flattered you find me so…"

"Enchanting. I find you utterly enchanting, and make no pretense otherwise." Nick ran his hand smoothly down her arm and took her elbow in a possessive hand. "I sincerely hope that when you assume the role of lady of the manor at our own home, you will take the position as much to heart as your mother obviously does. Now, it looks like we are being called to the dining room, darling."

Chapter 12

"There are few pleasures I enjoy as much as a country dance."

Lucie fanned her face with one hand, hoping to lose some of the glow she had achieved from the vigorous dance steps. The music had stopped, but the noise level in the crowded room had not diminished. Excitement at the impromptu round of dancing gave the post-dinner chatter a markedly festive air.

"Is that so?" Nick asked mildly. Despite wearing a starched shirt, cravat, vest and jacket, and having his legs encased in stockings and heavy breeches, he looked as fresh as if the dancing had just begun.

While the duke retained his cool demeanor, the musician was nearly done to a turn. They had been dancing for hours. It was well past midnight but no one seemed inclined to break up the party.

The French doors leading to the terrace stood wide open. Nick inclined his head and asked, "Shall we?"

She agreed immediately, without fear their leaving unchaperoned might cause unsavory gossip.

How different her circumstances had become. The last time she sought the night air at a dance, she had practically threatened Aunt Lucinda with a display of indelicate behavior if leave was not granted. Now, all she had to do was nod her head and she could take her leave without as much as a word of entreaty.

Freedom had never been an ideal Lucie associated with marriage. She was only now beginning to recognize its presence in the nuptial agreement.

"We are fortunate that your butler plays so well. It would have been unfortunate if we were in want of music with no one to provide it."

"Yes, that is true." She could have played the pianoforte, as could have either Amy or Miranda, but that would mean they would be forced to miss the dancing. It was better to allow Hastings entrance to the sitting room, and have him play in their stead.

Earlier she noticed her father setting a small glass of port on the edge of the instrument, near the keyboard, and encouraging the servant to take a sip. It was no surprise the man's fingers flew over the keys and the pace he set was exceedingly lively.

Nick placed his arm around her waist as he began to walk, giving her no choice but to go with him. Just a few days ago, walking in the dark of night, alone, with the duke would have filled her with trepidation. Now, however, Lucie had no fear of the man.

"The stars are beautiful, aren't they?" She tilted her head back to stare up into the velvety black sky. Points of light twinkled merrily above their heads. "When I was a child, I would come out here with Father and Oliver, and we would look at the stars for hours. I fell asleep so many times while we star-gazed that I stopped being shocked in the mornings when I woke up, not in a chair out here, but in my own bed."

"It is hard to imagine not being fascinated by the heavens, but there are some who never look up, and miss the wonder of this."

The dark brought them closer than daylight might

have. Nick's shoulder pressed hers, and his head and hers were nearly touching as they stared into the sky.

His nearness was enthralling. Lucie inhaled the faint scent of his aftershave. It had been overshadowed by the aroma of cigars and the musky, masculine scent of a man who had recently danced hard. Nick's body felt solid against her own, an anchor in the darkness. If she closed her eyes, she knew she would not fall, not even if, surrounded by the dark, she could not tell which was up and which down. She would not fall...because he was there. Finally, someone was beside her, ready to catch her if she stumbled.

"Have you a favorite constellation?" His voice was a low rumble that sent shivers along her spine.

"The Big Dipper. It was the first constellation I learned to find on my own, and while there are others— many others, of course—I find appealing, I cannot blithely hand over the Big Dipper for one of the more dazzling displays."

He chuckled, the sound low and rich. "So you are loyal? Is that it?"

"I am, especially where the Big Dipper is concerned." She turned to face him.

That was her first mistake. When they had been side by side, Lucie hadn't seen his face, hadn't been forced to look into Nick's eyes and hadn't been held captive by his stare. Now she was forced to do all three, and for the first time she felt the full weight of his feelings for her.

What have I done?

He slowly smiled. "There are none in the night sky who can outshine you. You bring them all to shame with your beauty, Lucie."

"That-that is kind of you to say...it is not necessary, however. You-you do not need to flatter me." She could not meet his eyes, so she stared at his cravat. It had been tied to the last pleat hours earlier. Now it looked less crisp, but it was still faultlessly fixed. Not even his neckwear wilted, while she felt positively limp.

He placed a fingertip beneath her chin and turned her head up. Their gazes met, and she saw he was not amused.

"You think I flatter you? That I am plying you with Spanish coin? Oh, darling, don't you know me better by now?" He arched an eyebrow. "Haven't you understood what I have been trying to tell you from the beginning? I do not engage in falsehoods, and that includes empty flattery."

"I thought you were just being kind."

"I am being honest." Nick stood so close that had they not been wed it would have been highly scandalous. "I will not insult you—*ever*—by saying what I do not believe, what I do not feel."

Then, her life changed yet again.

His kiss was tender, and her lips moved beneath his without any conscious effort. Then, remembering who she was and what she was doing, she went cold at his touch. She was not prepared for his advances, had not expected this. She pushed against Nick's chest with her palms. There was no need to push hard. As soon as she tried to pull away he released her.

"I will not do this." Confusion swirled inside her head, making it difficult to hold her wits. His touch had brought feelings she had not imagined she possessed.

"Will not do what? Kiss your husband?" Nick's

dark gaze slammed into her, forceful and direct. "You seem to forget that we are not acquaintances. I have not signed your dance card, and I do not need to ask permission to kiss my own wife. We are married, Lucie—or have you forgotten?"

His frustration could not be hidden. She had, for the first time in their short marriage, angered the man.

"I will not allow you to force yourself on me," she countered.

"You kissed me back. I know it is indelicate to point out, but it is the truth. When I kissed you, you responded—that is, until you realized what you were doing. That is, unfortunately, when you turned and ran like a startled rabbit."

"I am no rabbit. And I did not run! I am here, right here, exactly as I have been these last minutes." Their mouths were no longer connected, but their bodies were still very close. And to her chagrin, his observation was correct. She had kissed him back, if only momentarily. Moreover, the kiss had been heavenly.

But one kiss does not a marriage make. She could not forget herself, could not allow him to take what she was not willing to give. This was the moment she had been waiting for, the point where she would make herself perfectly clear on the point of marital familiarity.

Nick chuckled again, but this time there was a mocking tone to his voice.

"No? Well, my dear, you are doing an excellent imitation of a frightened bunny, then."

The cheek of the man! It did not matter that they had enjoyed an unforgettable day, that she had shared the Folly with him, or that their evening of dining and dancing had been the best in her lifetime. No, none of that seemed to matter to him. It was, apparently, not enough to satisfy him. He wanted—no he fairly demanded—more.

Lucie's resolve not to be pushed renewed itself.

She took a step back, putting some space between them. "Be that as it may, I am not frightened of you. Nor am I intimidated by your demeanor."

"Intimidated? It is not my intention to intimidate, darling." He took a step forward but Lucie took one back. They seemed engaged in a dance of their own making, one that required neither music nor other dancers. "I do not wish to scare you, or intimidate you, Lucie. I…I merely wish to love you."

Love? He dared speak of love?

Lucie brushed the notion aside. It was too difficult to bear consideration. Love was for those whose marriage was based upon its beauty. It should not be corrupted, or the notion basely tossed about, by those who had surrendered all hope for love in exchange for more mundane conveniences.

"I will not allow you to take…that is, you cannot take what I am not willing to give."

There. She had said it. The flattery, advances and even the kisses should end. There was no sense knocking on a locked door, one whose key had been hidden away.

"Am I to assume you are denying me all marital privileges? Is that what you are saying?"

"That is precisely what I am saying. It is better, I suppose, to finally have this subject out in the open, so we may deal with it and then, of course, forget it. There is no need to discuss an issue over and over again when the discussion will not lead anywhere. That is the truth, don't you think?"

He looked, by parts, dazed, confused, amused and annoyed by her words. Had she not seen it herself, all clearly in his eyes and on his face, Lucie would not have believed it possible to experience so many emotions in such a short period of time.

"*The truth?* You are kidding me—that is the only reasonable explanation I can conjure." Nick placed a hand on her upper arm, and pulled her gently to him. There was no force in his touch, only quiet tenderness, so she went willingly. "I cannot believe you are saying these things, Lucie. We are, I remind you yet again, husband and wife. Last night, I saw you were tired so I did not press the issue, but we cannot go on forever living like brother and sister. We are married, don't you understand that?"

His distress was apparent, so she did not have the heart to pull away from him. Standing so close, feeling his breath on her cheek and the warmth of his body heating hers simply by its proximity made thinking clearly nearly impossible, but Lucie was determined to keep her intellect intact. It was bad enough her body betrayed her; keeping her wits was paramount to surviving this conversation.

"I understand our marital status." She could not take much more of this. It hurt too much to admit aloud what she had so willingly done. The whole of her life, she would be sorry she had not married for love. But there was no helping it…the family had, and always would, come first.

Better to just say it and be done with it. Then we can go on, somehow…

Lucie met Nick's gaze full on. She did not allow herself to look away. He deserved her undivided attention.

"We both know we did not marry for…well, we did not marry for the usual reasons. And while I will always be in your debt for what you have done, I cannot forget that we did not marry for love. We are…oh, Nick! We have a marital arrangement—we both know it is so."

"But—"

"No, I cannot give my body to a man who has not claimed my heart. I will not—oh, Lord, I cannot."

Tears streamed down her face. She had no idea when they started, and only noticed them when he dashed a teardrop off her chin just before it fell onto her gown. She rushed on, not caring now about holding her voice steady and reasonable. The conversation had to be gotten through, once and for all. Perhaps then they could forget this night had ever taken place.

"My heart is all I have left, don't you understand? In all honesty, I know you can demand certain things of me, but I pray you do not."

"I would not force you. Don't you know me better than that?"

She stared into his eyes. Sadly, with a small shake of her head, she said, "I fear we do not know each other at all. Not yet, and maybe not ever. We have, for better or worse, entered into an arrangement. All I am saying is that I cannot compromise my soul further. I cannot freely give what has not been earned. I am sorry, Nick. I cannot give myself to a man without love. Ours must continue to be a marriage in name only. Please understand—"

He did not try to hold her back when she twisted out of his grip and turned away. With one last look into his disappointed face, she wiped her cheeks. Then, she did play the part of a rabbit and ran into the night.

It was all she could think to do, given the fact her heart felt like it was shattering into a million pieces, and scattering to the ends of the sky…just like the stars above her head.

Chapter 13

Nick was gone when Lucie went downstairs the next morning.

She had not heard any noise from his bedroom since shortly after she had closed—and locked—the connecting doors between their rooms. To her relief, he had not tried to gain access to her chamber. She had no delusions that a man of Nick's size and strength would be deterred by a locked door if he truly wanted to gain entrance. A small part of her regretted that he had not even jiggled the doorknob.

A brisk turn around the downstairs rooms, and onto the terrace, proved fruitless. He was nowhere to be found.

The hour was later than it had been yesterday, so perhaps he had gone riding or for a walk. She had dallied, not wanting to appear too early, and now wished she had not asked for a tray to be sent to her room. Had she come downstairs, she might have taken breakfast with more than just Cedric for company.

More from habit than anything else, Lucie turned toward the library. It was empty, dismally so. She remembered just a few days ago when she had come in search of a book to absorb her mind and had found, instead, Nick sitting in a chair reading Homer.

She dropped into the chair he had occupied, running a hand along the tufted arm and imagining his skin feeling this selfsame spot in the not-so-distant past.

During the long, restless hours of the previous night, Lucie had come to a momentous realization. Despite having wed the duke in order to help her family, she had, somewhere along the short journey, fallen in love with the man.

He was good and kind. His willingness to sacrifice his happiness for others was admirable beyond measure. He had left his own spacious home and was content to sleep beyond a locked door in his wife's home. His silence, holding salacious gossip-mongers at bay, kept her family intact. Nick had, most likely, saved her father's life. The stressful burdens he assumed in the older man's stead had improved an ailing heart.

In short, Lucie owed the lives of her family to the man—the man she loved, yet denied entrance to her bedchamber, as well as her heart. It made no sense, but it was, she thought with an ironic grin, the truth. Wasn't that all Nick had asked of her? The truth, in all things and at all times?

The truth...her heart was a traitor. Instead of holding fast to the businesslike arrangement she had convinced herself was her lot in life, her heart had given itself to the one man who had no illusions about their wedding.

He does not love me. He married me out of obligation to Father. That is all.

Despite her vow never to give herself fully to any man for whom she did not share a mutual love, during the long, restless night she had come to a conclusion she never imagined she would make. She had decided to allow Nick his marital rights. It seemed only fair. He had, after all, claimed her heart. And his goodness of heart should somehow be rewarded. His actions had been for the benefit of those around him. Lucie had decided it was time he benefit from the arrangement, as well.

Now, if she could only find the man to tell him the news.

As she grabbed *The Odyssey* from its familiar spot on the shelf, she wondered if finding one's husband was supposed to be this difficult a task.

What do I know? I am a married woman, in love with my husband, about to give myself to a man who does not love me. How can I know anything at all, if I do not know how to control my own thundering heart?

****

"You must come with me, Lucie. I will not quarrel over it, either. You must accompany me this very minute." His tone brooked no argument.

She put a sliver of grass between the pages of the book, then closed it and placed it on her lap. A green-checkered quilt spread on the ground beneath her, protecting her legs from all manner of biting insects while she read, her back resting against the trunk of the oak tree beneath which Nick had proposed marriage.

It seemed a logical spot to fritter away the hours. He had to return to the manor eventually, but she could not stand wandering from window to window, the way she had done all morning, watching for his arrival. Shortly before noon she had grabbed the quilt and her book and had come to the spot beside the greenhouse. When the head gardener witnessed her arrival, he had moved his pruning ministrations to the far side of the garden, leaving her in solitude. She was grateful, and as the hours passed Lucie was finally able to quell some of the turmoil roiling within her.

She hesitated—she knew he must be angry with her, but she had not realized he would be this furious. Looking up into his face, she saw a man who seemed quite at the end of his rope, both figuratively and literally. Never before had she seen Nick in such a state of dishevelment. His curls were mussed, his cravat askew and his usually shining Hessian boots bore traces of something red and sticky on them.

Good God, has he gone and murdered someone?

"I mean it. I will not argue over this. You will not talk your way out of this, and if you try to run, I will catch you." He spoke with enough force that she believed him. Nick squatted beside her, bringing his face level with hers. He had never looked this serious before, and the expression in his face was so fierce she was nearly frightened. Nearly, but not quite. Then, a grin pulled the edge of one lip upward. "If you try to bunny hop away from me, my dear Lucie, I will put you over my shoulder and carry you off. Mark my words, I will do it—and I will have no care to what anyone sees, hears, or thinks. Tongues may wag until they fly out of mouths, for all I care. Test me on this and you will see just how serious I am."

"I believe you. I will not run…not again. I have decided that last night was the only time I shall run from you, or from our problems. I am sorry to have taken such a cowardly way out of our discussion. It will not happen again."

Lucie swallowed hard. Enduring his scrutiny nearly drove her to distraction. She wanted desperately to look away, but she would not give herself the leeway to do so.

No more running. No more avoiding him. They were, as he said, married. If he did not love her, it would have to be enough that Lucie loved him.

"I am glad to hear that." A brisk nod brought a curl falling over one eye, giving him a rakish appearance. With surprisingly steady fingers, Lucie reached out and swept the lock off Nick's brow.

"I-I acted childishly. I am sorry for running from you." She shrugged and stared openly into his eyes. If he thought anything of her apology, he concealed it from her. There was no reading the man behind the dark eyes today. They were closed to her, so she went on blindly. "It was not an adult way to solve an issue. I fear I do not have much experience with men, and have certainly never encountered…ah, I have never had to consider issues such as we have between us."

"I am also glad to hear that," he said with a small grin.

Emboldened, Lucie returned the grin. "I spoke honestly, though. I meant what I said—I have never believed I would give myself fully to a man who does not love me. In truth, it never occurred to me I would marry for anything other than love." She took a deep breath, and then exhaled slowly, before she went on. "But, as you well know, that is exactly what I have done. You are right, we are married, and you are free to claim your rights as my husband." She met his gaze and said boldly, "I have heard that men who are denied their rights often seek their solace elsewhere. I do not want us to have a marriage of that sort."

Nick's grin vanished. He took her chin in his hand, and leaned so close she could smell mint on his breath. "That will never—I repeat, *never*—happen between us.

It is the reason I demanded honesty from you. It is the reason—"

He snapped his mouth shut, giving an exasperated groan. Nick sat back on his heels, holding his temples with both hands as if they pained him.

"What? What is the reason, Nick?"

He let his hands drop, and then met her gaze. "My parents have never been true to each other. They have…well, they have always been honestly dishonest with each other, if that makes any sense. They have never concealed their indiscretions, nor have they attempted to maintain a loyal, sincere association." He paused, staring into her eyes for a long, quiet moment. "That is one of the reasons I agreed to marry you. I recognized your truthful nature, and knew that even if our marriage did not begin with love we would, at the very least, share faithfulness and respect. It is more, I fear, than my parents have ever shared. So, Lucie, you do not have to fret that I will find solace elsewhere. I would rather live a solitary existence than bring dishonesty to our nuptial vows."

She steadied herself and spoke. "I am sorry. I had no idea."

"No one knows. It is—well, let us just say that every family has its secrets, shall we? And speaking of family secrets…you need to accompany me. I have something to show you. Together we must decide how to proceed."

Without waiting for her to reply, Nick grabbed her hands and pulled her to her feet as he stood. When they were nose to nose, he looked contemplatively into her eyes. It was the first time she felt connected to him since last night's dancing. It hit her then how much she had missed being this near to him.

Her heart recognized what her mind had taken so long to see. She loved him—and now that she realized it there could be no turning back. She would not humiliate herself further by admitting her feelings, but she would not—*could not*—deny the man she adored so fully any longer.

Just when she imagined life and the state of her marriage could not get any more muddled, she had done the unforgivable. She had lost herself to her husband. There was no turning back, no mistaking the truth.

The most she could hope to do was to hold onto her dignity, since Nick so unmistakably had possession of her heart.

Chapter 14

Lucie recognized the tiny, secluded cottage instantly. It was the one furthest from the manor house, the one least accessible by horse and almost entirely inaccessible by foot. It would have taken hours to reach the spot had they not ridden two of the finest animals from the stables.

The cottage should have been shuttered and closed up, with weeds growing over the mossy stepping stones leading to the curved front door. That was not the case, however. The windows were open wide, a gray curl of smoke lifted lazily from the stone chimney and there were no weeds at all in the yard. Footprints gouged the red mud beside the gate.

She remained, silent and still, on her saddle while Nick dismounted. He looped his horse's reins over a post in the shade of a weeping willow before he moved to stand beside her mount. When he held his arms out to her, she dropped the reins and fell into his grasp. The moment between horse and earth, when she was clasped in her husband's strong hands, made her head swirl. The feeling was delicious, but all too soon it was at an end.

"You are familiar with this cottage?"

"I have not been here in years, but yes, I am aware of it."

Nick blocked her from moving forward. She could

not fathom what he was doing. He had clearly brought her to the place with a purpose in mind. Why try to deter her now?

"There is something I must tell you, but it is not easy for me to say." His mouth and eyes softened, but his tone grew serious. "This may upset you, and I am sorry for that, but there is no help for it."

Her heart stirred. The emotion in his gaze moved her to speak impulsively.

"Whatever it is, just say it. Whatever you want, simply demand it. I have already made it clear to you that I will not deny you, Nick. There is no need for you to feel so badly about claiming what is already, by legal right and in God's eyes, yours."

He placed his hands on her shoulders, and drew her close enough that their breaths mingled. She stared into the deep recesses of his eyes, wondering what he was thinking. Too, she could not help but speculate on what, precisely, he would demand from her.

"You really believe me so barbaric that I would bring you all the way out here to exert my rights over you? What, do you imagine that I have brought you to a place where your screams will not be heard—is that it?"

"I will not scream. And I do not think you are barbaric...in fact, I am quite impressed with your...ah, with your manners and restraint."

Nick heaved a full sigh as a small smile turned his lips. "Well that is something, at least."

"So what now?" Tension held her like a coiled spring. "We are here...what is the plan?"

"Right to the point, aren't you? Well, despite your tantalizing offer of..." Nick raked his gaze down her body, then up again before he met her own wide stare.

"Well, despite the offer, we have not come here to consummate our marriage. And, as I said a minute or so ago, what I have to tell you may hurt you. I am sorry—"

The waiting was killing her. "But it cannot be helped. What is it? Just tell me the truth, and be done with it."

"Oliver is in the cottage. I have spent the day here with him, and he is aware that I went back to the manor to fetch you here. His is the matter that I told you we need to resolve. He is waiting to see you."

With all that had gone on during the past half-day, she had almost forgotten about her mad brother. The topic was one she, to her supreme chagrin, tried to overlook at every possible turn because Nick was right: Oliver as a subject wrenched her heart so severely it left her out of breath.

"Is he...is he all right? I mean, is he all right enough that I may visit with him?"

Nick seemed resigned. "He is fine. In fact, he is more up to the visit than either you or I may be. Come, shall we go inside so you may see for yourself?"

Lucie shot around him and ran up the walk. He followed close on her heels—so close, in fact, that when she stopped at the open doorway he ran smack-dab into her.

Together they tumbled through the door, nearly falling to their knees as they gripped each other tightly and laughed over the absurdity of their situation.

A deep voice halted the laughter. "That is, by far, one of the most intriguing entrances I have ever seen."

Oliver looked, and sounded, himself. A bit whiter than she remembered, and somewhat thinner, but still, it was Oliver. Her heart surged at the sight of him. Hearing him speak in a normal tone of voice, instead of the insane ranting she had heard last from him, filled her with unbridled joy.

Opening her arms wide, she flew to embrace her brother. He anticipated the movement and grabbed her in a warm hug. For an instant her toes left the ground, and it was like the past weeks had never even happened.

When they separated, Lucie turned to Nick. "You knew this? You knew he is—that he can—that he is not—"

"A raving lunatic? Yes, I knew." Nick nodded and, when no one else moved from the spot just inside the open front door, he shouldered the door closed and motioned toward the small sitting room that lay beyond. "Shall we?"

She turned to Oliver, hoping to still see him smiling and in control of himself. In the seconds her attention had been on Nick, she feared her brother might revert to the madman whose screams still rang in her ears.

As if sensing her unspoken question, Oliver smiled. Then he swept an arm out, also urging her into the next room. Speechless, Lucie walked between them. The room was sparsely, but suitably, furnished. She dropped to a side chair, glad for its presence because her knees suddenly felt shakier than usual.

The men sat, and then exchanged glances.

She took charge of the conversation. "So, you knew that Oliver is not…ill."

Nick sighed. "Today, when I arrived I knew. Actually, before now I suspected."

"Suspected what?" Lucie turned an anxious face on her brother. She held out a hand, palm up, beseechingly. "Oliver, what did Nick suspect? What is going on—someone must tell me!"

"Nick knew what I could not admit to anyone, my dear sister," Oliver said with such sadness that it nearly broke her heart to hear him. "I could not—no, I *would not* tell anyone the truth before your husband threatened me with—"

Lucie whirled to face Nick, horror making her move more quickly than she ever had before. "You threatened my brother? How in the world could you do such a thing? My God, what did you threaten to do to the poor, sick man?"

His brows lifted. "I threatened to have him committed to the Hospital of Saint Mary of Bethlehem—"

"Bedlam!"

"That is correct. I told Oliver I would send him to Bedlam unless he told me the truth about his illness. In short, darling, I threatened to have your brother thrown into an asylum filled with all the other barmy Englishmen."

"You did not!"

"I did." Nick grinned, as if he were proud of attempting to have her brother locked up.

Lucie turned to Oliver for confirmation. He, too, looked satisfied with what had transpired.

"Oliver? Please, tell me what is going on here. I cannot bear not knowing, when whatever has happened has obviously done you so much good. Tell me, are you truly as well as you appear or is this an illusion? I am not certain I could bear the latter, but I must know for certain."

"I am fine, Lucie, perfectly fine. Stupid and embarrassed, remorseful and somewhat worse for the wear, but I have learned a very valuable lesson. It nearly cost me my life and all I hold dearest, but it is a mistake I will never make again." Oliver looked solemnly into her shocked eyes. "I swear to you, I will never again do what I have done, never again disgrace the family or cause one instant of worry to our parents. I will never be able to adequately thank you and Nick for sacrificing your happiness, and your futures, on my account."

Nick leaned forward and put his elbows on his knees. Threading his fingers together, he looked into Lucie's eyes. "Do you understand what Oliver is trying to say? I want you to know precisely what we are dealing with here, so that we three may decide on a course of action."

"I admit, I am not entirely certain. How could he be out of his mind one minute and sane the next? It does not make sense."

"Oh, but it does." Nick shot a fast glance at Oliver, who nodded his accord, before he went on. "You see, Oliver picked up some rather unsavory habits while he was abroad. He began to use…substances which were not entirely healthy. Do you understand now what we are attempting to tell you?"

Horror spread through Lucie like an uncontrolled wildfire. It filled her with its intensity, and fury, and she slapped a hand on the arm of her chair.

Turning to Oliver, she asked, "Is Nick saying you used medicinal brews—for non-medicinal purposes?"

Her brother nodded, his shame as plain as the nose

on his face. "He is. And he is correct. And I am...oh, Lucie I am sorry. When I realized my mind was compromised, and I could not control the monster that clung to my back like a rabid monkey, I swore my valet to secrecy, and asked he bring me home to Willowbrook Manor.

"Of course, when Father asked what was wrong, he would not give me up, so our parents assumed I went crazy. I knew that if I could keep myself away from the mixture it would, eventually, leave my body. It was a living nightmare, to expel the demons I had created within myself, but I have done it. I promise, dear sister, I am fully restored. I am myself again, and I will be forevermore. You must believe me, please."

He shoved a hand through his hair, sending the wavy brown locks into a mess of hills and valleys. The motion was familiar, something he had done as a small boy and a gesture that now brought Lucie to tears. They were tears of joy, and relief, and once they began they did not stop for a very long time.

****

It was dark by the time the trio returned to the manor house. They had all agreed Lord and Lady Gregory had already suffered enough to learn the truth about Oliver's affliction. Nick and Oliver had already formulated an excuse that was, in part, true and which would, in its entirety, solve the issues surrounding the heir to Willowbrook and the duke's title. Lucie had only to agree, and the secret would be kept.

When she looked askance at her husband, clearly shocked he might consider even a small subterfuge within his realm of possibilities, Nick shrugged and gave a resigned grin.

"There are, I am forced to admit, times in life when total honesty seems cruel. Your parents do not need to know about their son's medicinal addiction. It would serve no purpose. And since Oliver did fall into a case of the blue-devils as he worked through the affliction, telling them he suffered from serious depression seems enough of the truth to satisfy everyone."

Their arrival brought tears of joy from both parents. Oliver's restoration made Lord Gregory seem even hardier than he had been only that morning, and the lady of the manor looked positively glowing as she gazed adoringly on her son.

Lucie and Nick told the truth when asked to remain in the parlor, and celebrate Oliver's homecoming. They were tired, worn out from the day's activities, and desired to retire to their suite. The declaration was met with knowing grins and raised eyebrows.

Lady Gregory declared she would arrange to have their supper sent upstairs so they would not have to venture out of their rooms before morning.

In the hallway outside her bedroom door, Lucie stood and debated how to proceed. She had made an oath before her friends, family, God and Nick, and intended to finally make good on her words. But she was so disheveled, and reeked of sweaty horse, that she could not imagine feeling even the tiniest bit romantic in her current state.

Nick solved her dilemma. He walked past her, and then stopped at his own chamber door.

"I am in dire need of hot water and soap. If you will excuse me while I bathe, I will meet you back in our sitting room in a short time. I imagine your mother has ordered the cook to send up enough food to feed an army. I must confess, I am hungry enough to eat like a starving battalion. Does the arrangement sound agreeable to you? Or are you, perhaps, too worn out to dine with me?"

His solicitude warmed her, and erased some of the weariness from her body. He cared how she felt, and what she thought. Even if he did not love her, he cared for her. That was, she realized, more than enough.

"I would love to dine with you. And if we are being perfectly frank, I think I may be able to out-eat your battalion. I would love the opportunity to clean up first, though. As soon as I am ready, I will meet you in our sitting room."

She turned the doorknob and would have gone into her room except that she felt Nick's gaze still on her. Turning to face him, she asked, "What is it? Have I mud splattered on my face that I am not aware of?"

The ploy worked. Nick's stare had been somber. At her teasing, he smiled, and hurried to assure her, "No mud. I was just thinking that I am looking forward to a nice, quiet meal with my wife."

My wife. It was the first time he had used the phrase so familiarly.

Lucie fought to control her emotions. "As am I, with my husband."

She opened the door and hurried through, too flustered by her own nerve to look back at his expression.

****

The cook had outdone herself on the meal. There was enough roasted partridge, Welsh rarebit, and white soup on their dinner cart to feed an additional starving battalion. The couple ate their fill, lingering over figs and cheese as the fire burned low in the hearth.

Lucie had never felt this completely at ease with anyone. It was a new, and exhilarating, experience. She would not allow herself to contemplate what might happen after every morsel on their plates had been consumed.

I will simply trust him. Whatever comes next...comes next.

Whatever she had expected to happen was inconsequential. When Nick, seated beside her on a chintz sofa before the fire, turned to face her his expression was serious.

He does not want me, she thought. I have offered myself to him, but it does not matter. He is too much a gentleman to demand what is his.

"I have given this a great deal of contemplation, Lucie. In fact, for the past day I have not thought of much else." Nick stretched out an arm along the sofa back. "The truth of it is, you are willing to act in a matrimonial manner, even if it means you must do what you do not wish to do. I, however, cannot allow that to happen. It would not be—"

He stopped, and for a moment she feared he would not finish. Then he said, "It would not be right if I forced myself on you. I could not do that to a woman I do not care for. I certainly cannot—*and will not*—do it to someone I love."

Her ears deceived her! Surely he could not have proclaimed his love—could he?

"You-you...oh, say it again. Tell me I have not taken leave of my senses." Words fell over each other as she tried to make sense of what he had said. "Please, tell me again..."

Nick pulled his brows high on his forehead, disbelief shining brightly in his eyes. "You mean you did not suspect I have fallen in love with you? Lucie, but I thought I was so transparent as to have seemed foolish." He sighed, and then said, "It is the whole truth, I swear it. I love you, Lucie Grayson. There is no disputing that, but it still does not change the fact that even though I adore you I will not force you—"

"I love you, Nick," she whispered.

His mouth hung open in shock, so she said it again.

"I love you. I cannot help it. Your honor, integrity, sense of humor, kindness…oh, all of it…you have won me over. Claimed my heart."

He studied her seriously while her heart thudded wildly. It was astounding that an organ could pound so hard and not be heard.

Then, wordlessly, he kissed her and this time she did not pull away. The moment was magical and sealed their fates.

When Nick rose, he swept Lucie into his arms and held her close against his chest. For the first time in her life, she knew she was in the exact spot that had been destined for her—and only her. She would never regret any bit of what led them to this moment, nor would she have remorse over whatever lay before them. Whatever destiny had in store for Lord and Lady Grayson, they would meet it all head on—together.

He walked to the doorway leading into her bedchamber. Then, he stopped and gave her the handsomest smile she had ever seen.

"What do you say, darling? Are you ready to leave this part of our lives behind and cross over the threshold into the next chapter of our marriage?"

"As long as I am with you, Nick, I am ready for anything."

A word about the author...

Sarita Leone loves adventure, whether it be in a distant continent or her own backyard. When she's not off exploring the world, she keeps busy writing, reading, and dancing beneath the stars. Always a fan of happy endings, she's fortunate to have a job which allows for so many of those!

She loves to hear from readers. Easiest way to connect? Check out her Facebook page, where all the latest news hits the screen.

Thank you for purchasing
this publication of The Wild Rose Press, Inc.

If you enjoyed the story, we would appreciate your
letting others know by leaving a review.

For other wonderful stories,
please visit our on-line bookstore at
www.thewildrosepress.com.

For questions or more information
contact us at
info@thewildrosepress.com.

The Wild Rose Press, Inc.
www.thewildrosepress.com

Stay current with The Wild Rose Press, Inc.

Like us on Facebook

https://www.facebook.com/TheWildRosePress

And Follow us on Twitter
https://twitter.com/WildRosePress

www.ingramcontent.com/pod-product-compliance
Lightning Source LLC
Chambersburg PA
CBHW071311200626
46813CB00015B/1523